THE
GIRL
IN THE
LAKE

THE GIRL IN THE LAKE

INDIA HILL BROWN

Scholastic Press
New York

Library of Congress Cataloging-in-Publication Data available
ISBN 978-1-338-67888-8

1 2021
Printed in the U.S.A. 23
First edition, January 2022
Book design by Maeve Norton

FOR MY COUSINS, ESPECIALLY THE ONES
WHO HAVE GRADUATED FROM THE
KIDS' TABLE.

CHAPTER 1

Every time Grandma Judy or Grandad Jim called, whether it was to wish us happy birthday or Merry Christmas or just to talk with Mama, they'd always make us promise to come visit their lake house "next summer."

"Next summer" is finally here. Just a couple of weeks after I failed my last swimming lesson.

I don't think that's a coincidence, either. Grandma Judy and Grandad Jim are huge on everyone in our family loving the water and learning how to swim. So of course, when I fail my swimming lesson and decide I won't be swimming again, it's the summer we actually visit the lake house.

"You can't fail a swimming lesson, Celeste," my dad tells me after I failed it. But as a dad, he's supposed to say that. My brother, Owen, learned really fast, and he's ten and I'm twelve. But at the end of my last lesson, I still didn't know how to swim, which seems like failing to me.

I told my dad afterward that I don't want to swim anymore, but I should have known better than to say that.

"You know how important swimming is to our family," Mama said. Her dad, Grandad Jim, was a lifeguard. Mama says she's been swimming for so long, she doesn't even remember learning. Dad was afraid of swimming until after he married Mama, when she convinced him to finally learn, so I thought he'd understand how hard it was. But instead he says, "If I can learn, you can learn."

I think I get my swimming genes from Dad, because every time my instructor, Stinky-Breath Jared, told me to jump into his arms, I'd freeze up. Eventually, he'd get annoyed.

I did *not* like Jared with the Stinky Breath. He sighed way too many times when I wasn't brave enough to jump into his arms in the swimming pool. Like I was taking too long. But I didn't get it. For the next forty minutes, he didn't have anywhere else to be. Why was he rushing me?

He pronounced my name wrong, too. He would always say it like "Cel-es-tee." Until I worked up the nerve to correct him.

"It's Cel-*lest*," I finally told him, staring at my reflection in the rippling blue water.

"Just come on," he said. I could tell he was getting annoyed. "You can do it. It's not that hard."

I didn't have the guts to tell him that it *was* that hard for me. I wanted to tell him that my name wasn't that hard to pronounce, either, but he kept messing that up, and I'd never jumped in a body of water before. I wanted to tell him that since he seemed so annoyed with me, I didn't trust him to catch me if I messed up. So I didn't say anything.

Just forget it, I thought to myself.

I wouldn't move an inch closer to the water. I just stood there, smelling the chlorine. One time I heard someone giggle and it was a toddler. She had on a swimsuit that was made to look like a strawberry. She was laughing at me. Then she jumped into her own daddy's arms in the pool without a care in the world.

After that last lesson, I suggested that my daddy teach me how to swim instead. I'd feel way more comfortable jumping into his arms than Stinky-Breath Jared's. Or Mama's, since she's so good at it.

"Grandad will teach you," she told me. Then she stopped herself and says, "Grandad *can* teach you." After she said this, she asks Owen and me how we'd feel about spending the week with our grandparents and cousins. And that lets me know that's the whole reason we're going to the lake house this summer.

———————

Now I'm in the car with my mom, my dad, and Owen, on the way there. It used to be a place where my mom and her brothers and sisters would play and swim all summer long with our grandparents. Then when my grandparents stopped working, they moved there full-time. I love our grandparents, but since we moved a little farther away, we don't see them as much. Our cousins will be there, too. They are from different states and I haven't seen them in a couple of years. I just remember Capri being bossy and Daisy being quiet.

Owen must realize we're getting closer, because he finally stops telling us every single fact he knows about trees, lakes, and hiking trails and just stares out the window. If Grandma and Grandad were going to make me swim, then they were probably going to make Owen hike, too. My brainiac brother is usually totally logical, but for some reason hiking is the one thing he's really afraid of.

Our car bounces up and down on a dirt road, the trees closing in on either side of us. I never knew a road could be so bumpy. We pass a town library, a small grocery store, and then pretty soon, I don't see much of anything except for houses every now and then.

"We're here," Mama says. She turns around and smiles at me and Owen in the back seat. I try to return her smile. Mama always talks about how she and her brothers and sisters—my aunts and uncles—loved to come here and swim when they were younger. I guess she thinks it's going to be the same with me and my cousins.

We pull up to a big white house with black shutters. I can see the lake peeking out from behind the house, sparkling in the sun. It's a beautiful setting, but seeing the water makes my stomach flip. There's a window at the very top of the house—I guess it's the attic. As I'm looking, I see something shine from the attic window, like a shadow with a really bright outline. *What is that?* I wonder. It's probably just the sunlight glinting off the glass.

"There's Grandma and Grandad!" Mom exclaims happily. "And there are your cousins." She points to the group of people clustered near the door. "They can't wait to see you. And look at my brothers and sisters! Let's go say hello."

We step out of the car and stretch the achiness out of our limbs. Even with the cool breeze coming from the lake, it's definitely hotter here than it is back home. Mama can't hide her grin as she and Daddy walk over to my aunts and uncles.

I see my uncle Howard getting bags out of a car parked right in front of ours, so I guess my cousin Capri is just getting here, too.

My eyes land on Capri. Her legs are twice as long as they were the last time I saw her, and the muscles in her calves are twice as big. I know her sixteenth birthday is coming up this fall. She'll probably be taller than Uncle Howard next year. She does not look like someone who "can't wait" to see me. She walks from behind Uncle Howard's car in some slouchy jean shorts that are just the right color blue, have the right amount of rips, aren't too tight, too loose, or too long. Her braids hang down her back and she's wearing gold hoop earrings, the really big ones that Mama won't let me wear yet. She's busy doing something on her phone and then I see her suck her teeth—probably when she realizes there is no cell phone service out here. I already realized that in the car.

Then there's my cousin Daisy. She is standing beside my aunt Marlene and uncle Steve wearing a white sundress with big red polka dots on it. She has an old-timey look, like she just stepped out of a black-and-white film. She always has—especially in her baby pictures, when she stared into the camera with her big round eyes. She has fluffy, bouncy curls and perfect posture, and looks straight ahead as she walks. Not down.

Almost like she's floating through the air. I could bet money no one ever told her to "sit up straight." She's kind of old-fashioned; she likes record players and stuff. Sometimes my dad would joke and say, "She seems like she's been here before." Whatever that means.

Owen and I walk over to them.

Daisy looks up, her hair blowing in the wind.

"Hello," she says. She is eleven, a year younger than me. She sounds so formal, like we aren't all cousins who used to play together a lot when we were little. But maybe that's just her personality.

"Hi," Owen and I say in unison.

She stares at us, taking us in. Her eyes feel like they're looking straight through me, like she can tell what I'm feeling.

"Owen and Celeste have grown a whole foot since I've seen them!" Uncle Howard's voice booms over ours as he laughs. He looks and sounds just like Grandad.

"Haven't they? And look at Capri's long legs! They will definitely get that Hawthorne height, that's for sure," Mama says, laughing as she hugs her brother.

"I've heard you've learned how to swim, Owen!" Howard slaps Owen on the back as a sign of congratulations. Owen smiles a little, glancing at me before he says, "Yeah."

"Don't worry, Celeste. Between that beautiful lake and the pool up the road, you'll be swimming in no time. Maybe Capri can drive you—"

Mama clears her throat and Capri glares at her dad. Then she glares at me. *What did I do?* Uncle Howard is sweating as if he's said something he shouldn't say. Or maybe he's sweating because it's so hot out here.

"Daisy, I love your dress," my mom says, trying to change the subject.

"Thank you," she says. She does a curtsy, like a girl out of a fairy-tale book, and Capri scoffs while Owen and I look at each other. Who does that?

"This girl. Straight out of the past," Aunt Marlene says. She gives Daisy's shoulder a squeeze.

We stand there as our parents talk and laugh with our aunt and uncles for a while, then they say their good-byes.

"Have the best time," Mama says, giving Owen and then me a huge hug. She and Dad look genuinely sad to go. Maybe they should stay here and us kids should go back to our houses, since they have so much fun here.

"My girl. Call me if you need anything," Dad says. He winks, and somehow I know he's talking about swimming. So I think he gets it. But it's not that I'm afraid of swimming, exactly. At first it sounded fun, but my swimming instructor made it kind of difficult for me, and now I just don't care anymore. Maybe he was right, it wasn't that hard, and I was just being silly. And not to mention, right after failing, I had a nightmare about falling into a big body of water. It felt so real and now I'm definitely not in a rush to learn how to swim.

"Okay," I say, hugging him, too.

Capri walks over to us, a scowl on her face. Daisy, Owen, and I all say hi to her, but she just waves us off. I sigh. I don't want to have to deal with her attitude all week. I always thought Capri was pretty bossy, anyway. I don't get it. When I'm at home, I'm the oldest and I don't boss Owen around at all.

We wave as the grown-ups pile into their cars and then disappear, one by one, until all that's left is an old Ford pickup truck and a Jeep. Grandma and Grandad's cars.

I peek around the back of the house to the wide, green backyard. The trees have branches that hang really low and create long shadows across the grass. They back into a wooded area that looks worn down with tire tracks. I wonder if Grandad drives through there to get to town. I wonder if that's where Grandma and Grandad hike. I wonder what's back there.

I look around some more. I see the deck that leads to the lake.

I can't help but admit to myself that the lake is beautiful, with its deep blue and the glitter from the sun. But it's so big, it overwhelms me. It's at least ten times bigger than the pool. Will Grandad make me jump in the lake? I hope not. It's pretty to look at, but the thought of jumping in makes me feel dizzy.

Owen, Capri, Daisy, and I stand in awkward silence, staring at the house, the sparkling lake behind it.

"Come on in," Grandma says. She has a wide smile and nose like Mom.

We walk into the house and it's like all the hot air outside is packed into it. My forehead is still sweaty from standing outside. Their house smells different from our house. It makes a lot of noises, too, lots of creaks and groans. As soon as I walk in, the house sighs really loudly; it almost sounds like a voice saying, *"Hiiii."* We all stare at the ceiling. Grandma must see our expressions, because she tells us that it's just the "house settling in," whatever that means.

"All of your rooms are upstairs," Grandma says. "You can choose the ones you want and unpack, then come back downstairs for supper."

I already know which one I want: the one with the best view of the lake. Just because I don't want to swim in it doesn't mean I don't want to draw the view.

I run upstairs and into the room on the far left, eager to get the one with the biggest balcony before Capri does. The sun is setting just outside my window, the big oak tree casting a shadow that looks like a big hand over the room.

The floor creaks when I step inside, like the rest of this house. The bed looks comfortable, though, and there is a huge colorful quilt on the bed. The only things in here are a nightstand, a lamp, a dresser, the bed, and the quilt. I decide to put some things around the room, to make it feel more like home since it *will* be my home for the next week. I put a picture that my friends and I took at my friend Iris's summer slumber party on the dresser, with my sketch pad and colored pencils right beside it.

I told Iris about Stinky-Breath Jared and how he made me feel. She told me that I should've told him right then and there.

"You should've told him just like this!" she said, standing up with her beaded braids clanking together. "'First of all, my name is *Celeste*. I've never swum before and that's why it's hard. Duh! And your stinky breath isn't making it any easier. Stop acting annoyed with me and be patient!' And then when you *did* jump in, you could've splashed him." She giggled at the last part.

I just laughed and shook my head. I'm not like Iris. Sometimes it's hard for me to say what I feel.

I unroll my picture of Simone Manuel, the Olympic gold medalist swimmer, and stick it on the wall with a roll of tape I found at the bottom of my bag. I hope that she will inspire me to gather up the nerve to at least *jump* in the pool this summer.

I look around the room and try to get used to it. Even though it's so old, it still feels new to me. And quiet. And hot. The warm air is so thick, it makes the room feel crowded, like someone is in here with me. I look around, twice, even though I know I'm the only person in here. I open a window to let some air in.

I hear a knock at the door. "It's time for dinner," someone says, and then I hear feet running away. The voice is strangely old-fashioned—Daisy, I guess.

"Coming," I call. I go back into the hallway, the floor still creaking under my feet.

The door slams behind me.

I jump. Then I remember I left the window open. Sometimes at home when I leave the window open, my bedroom door slams, too.

I hear low giggling behind one of the doors and stop for a second to listen. It's probably Daisy again. Or maybe Capri got her phone to work.

I shake my head. I keep stopping and looking around

at random things. I just need to let myself get used to this house and new-to-me bedroom.

I walk downstairs. When I reach the door to the kitchen, I see everyone in the house is already sitting at the dinner table, settled in.

That's weird, I think. Then who's upstairs laughing? I guess it's just more creaking noises from this old lake house.

"Oh, Celeste! That's funny, I thought you were already down here." Grandma furrows her brows together, looking around at the dinner table, as if she sees me sitting there.

"Me too," says Daisy. She looks at the same empty seat that Grandma looks at.

"I was upstairs, starting to unpack," I say, sitting in the chair between Daisy and Owen. I look at Daisy. "I thought . . ." But I don't finish because Grandma is placing the last dish on the table.

Grandma looks around at us and smiles. "Who's hungry? I made a big dinner and a pitcher of fresh lemonade for us to enjoy."

My stomach growls in response. I hold Daisy's and

Owen's hands as Grandad leads grace. After we say amen, I help myself to the dinner spread around the table and try to decide what to start with. I pick up an ear of sweet corn and bite into it.

"Capri, I hear congratulations are in order," Grandad says, a twinkle in his eye.

Capri looks up, her frown replaced by surprise.

"Your father told me you're the new track team captain!"

"Thanks." She smiles, but then frowns again, like she just remembered something. She goes back to eating her food.

"Y'all eat up and sleep good tonight," Grandad says, looking around the table at us. He is super tall with a big booming voice and a gray beard. I haven't seen that smile in a little while, but I've missed it. "There's so much for us to do this week!"

"Like what?" Capri grumbles. Her phone is lying beside her on the table, untouched. I guess she gave up on trying to get cell service. There's no Wi-Fi here, either.

"Why, all types of things!" Grandad opens his arms wide, his voice getting loud across the table. "For starters, we have a lake. Good for boating and swimming!"

He looks at me and winks. I smile back and put my head down, a little embarrassed. I know I'm the only person at the table who can't swim. I just know that Mama set this trip up so I could learn.

Owen clears his throat. "A boy at school told me that he never knew Black people had their own lake houses and he didn't believe me when I said you had one. He still thought I was making it up. I can't wait to show him photos of this place when I get back home."

I take another bite out of my corn on the cob, trying to stay silent, but the crunch is too loud. I glare at Owen, trying to get him to stop talking about swimming and water, but once he gets started, he can't be stopped.

He's still babbling. "He said it doesn't make sense for us to have our own lake houses because most Black people can't . . . swim." And that's when he looks up at me and gives me an apologetic smile.

Too late now, Owen. I continue eating my corn on the cob.

Grandad takes a bite of chicken and wipes his mouth off with his napkin. He looks straight at Owen. "You tell that fellow to learn his history. There's a reason a lot of Black people don't know how to swim. There was a time when Black people weren't even allowed in public pools. Do you all know the famous actress Dorothy Dandridge?"

Owen shakes his head, Capri shrugs with a frown, and Daisy gasps. "Oh, I love her!" she says. She's so quiet, I'd almost forgotten she's here.

"She was a legendary entertainer. And legend has it that an entire pool was drained at a Las Vegas hotel that she was supposed to perform at, because she stuck her toe in it. Can you imagine?"

"So Black people can't swim because they wouldn't let Dorothy Dandridge stick her foot in a pool at a hotel?" Capri asks, still frowning. I stare at her. I wonder what her problem is. She acts tough, but I can tell she really wants to know.

"It's more than that," Grandma says. "Once, Dr. King was arrested for integrating a restaurant at a motel. Peaceful protesters decided to wade into the motel pool to support him. Do you know that the pool owner poured acid in the pool while the protesters were inside it?" She shakes her head. Owen's eyes are wide. I know he can't wait to tell his friends this later.

"When my sister and I were younger, so many pools had Whites Only signs on them," Grandma continues. "How could we possibly learn to swim? If we tried at all, we had to swim in rivers and that could be dangerous. Years of not being allowed in pools or having the police being called on us for simply *being* in a pool, we rarely had the opportunity to learn. So we weren't able to pass that knowledge, or the simple joy of having fun in the water on the weekends, to our kids. All we could pass was the fear of the water or getting in trouble for something we just wanted to enjoy. So your classmate was right, in a way, that many Black people can't swim. But it's important that you know why, and that we work to change that. After Ellie—"

She stops, looks at Grandad, and sticks her fork into her macaroni and cheese. The sudden pause makes all of us look up, including Capri.

"Ellie?" Capri asks.

"Celestine. Your Great-Aunt Ellie," Grandma says.

"Oh," I say. That's who I'm named after. My full name

is Celeste Anne Cooper. I love my name because it's fun to draw lots of swirls around the *C*'s and the *E*'s. My great-aunt was named Celestine Johnson. I know that everyone called her Ellie for short, but I don't have a nickname. I'm just Celeste. I'm reminded again of the swimming instructor—always getting my name wrong, then asking me to jump in the pool. How could I trust someone to catch me when they couldn't even pronounce my name right?

"What about Great-Aunt Ellie?" Owen asks.

"Nothing, baby." Grandma shakes her head. I know she died when Grandma was younger. I guess it still hurts for her to talk about her.

"Your grandmother wanted to make it her duty to get her entire family swimming," Grandad continues. "That's how we met, you know. I was a lifeguard at the local community pool and she came to learn. Love at first swim." They exchange a smile.

I'm still eating all this good food, but I can't help but feel a little guilty. All Grandma's ever wanted is for her grandchildren to learn how to swim, and here I am, failing at swimming lessons.

"You look just like her. You know that?" Grandma says. I look up and she's staring right at me.

"Me?" I glance at Owen and he shrugs.

Grandma is still staring at me and I don't know what to say. I've never even seen a picture of Great-Aunt Ellie before, so I don't know if I really look like her. People say I look like Owen, but we only have the same eyes, Mom's hazel-brown eyes. Otherwise, I don't see it.

It's like Grandma reads my mind, because she asks me if I'd like to see a picture of her.

"I'll bring out the photo album after dinner," Grandma says. She wipes her mouth with a napkin and smiles. "She's the reason your grandfather built this place for me."

As the conversation moves on, I finish my food. I'm stuffed and ready for the first night in my new bed. Grandma puts a sweet potato pie on the table for dessert, but I don't know if I can eat a bite more. Owen, of course, takes a piece and puts it on one of the small dishes Grandma brought out.

Grandma disappears and comes back with a big

black book. She wipes some crumbs off the table before she gently places it down. Grandad steps behind Grandma and looks over her shoulder. Daisy scoots her chair closer to the table and Capri leans in.

We flip through some pictures I've seen copies of before, of my mom and aunts and uncles, running around under fire hydrants, playing in the pool, diving off the diving board, fishing and smiling in canoes.

Grandma smiles really big, looks at me, and hands me the photo album. "There she is. My big sister, Celestine," she says. "Have a look."

I look, ready to say something polite about how pretty she is or how nice she probably was. But when I see the picture, I scream. My heart beats fast and I hear Owen yell, Daisy squeal, and even Capri gasps.

I'm looking at a picture of myself.

CHAPTER 2

Owen jumps up. "Celeste!" he whispers. "Celeste, that's—that's you!"

It's silent as we all stare at the picture. It looks like me, frozen in time, in a black-and-white photo.

But it also *doesn't* look like me. Great-Aunt Ellie is standing with a big smile and a hand on her hip, in a frilly dress and a hat to match. It looks like she's standing outside a chapel. She has a sneaky smile on her face like she just played a joke on someone and they don't know it yet. It's not an expression I would make or an outfit I would wear, so it's weird to look at this person who's not me but looks exactly like me.

"That's creepy," Capri says. She gets closer to the photo album and her braids scratch the side of my face. I thought she'd say "Excuse me," but she doesn't.

"She's not creepy, she's your great-aunt," Grandma says defensively. She closes the photo album. I think she's upset that we all seem creeped out by her sister. "You all are being silly."

"Grandma?" I ask. "What happened to her?"

Grandma looks at me for a long time, like she's debating telling me. Then she shakes her head.

"We shouldn't talk about that right now."

What does that mean? I can't be too young; I just turned twelve. I wonder if Capri had asked, would she have told her? Maybe I just shouldn't have asked at all.

Daisy keeps staring at the photo album, even though it's closed. She looks at me. "Did it feel like you were looking in a mirror?"

"No," I answer her. But then I think about mirrors and how whenever you look at them, everything is the wrong way.

"Actually, yeah, I guess it did."

We all say good night and go back to our rooms. The lamp isn't on and it's dark now, so I have to feel my way around, my hand sliding over the quilt, until I reach the nightstand and turn on the lamp. It really is pitch-black out here. I walk to the window and look outside, expecting not to see anything, but instead I see more stars in the sky than I've ever seen. It has to be a million. Ten million, or even more. Of course we see stars back home, but never this many.

I crawl into bed. I'm sleepy, but I can't fall asleep. I keep thinking about that picture of Great-Aunt Ellie. I've never seen someone who looks exactly like me. Not even my mom, dad, or Owen.

I grab my sketch pad and pencils. I do a rough sketch of the navy-blue sky, mixing in blacks and light blues, adding a bunch of white and yellow dots around it for the stars. I love sketching. It helps me relax and get all the thoughts out of my head before I go to bed.

I hear a creak. It makes me think about earlier, when the house creaked when I stepped into this bedroom and how I thought I heard someone call me for dinner.

There are more groans and creaks, one directly above me. The attic? I think about how I thought I saw movement in the attic window when we drove up this afternoon, like someone was quickly walking by. How the house groaned as soon as I walked through the door.

I shake my head. I saw a shadow. Old houses creak.

I mess up on my drawing and accidentally sketch a yellow scribble of light through the air. I fix it quickly by making it into a shooting star. That's what I love about drawings. Even when they're sloppy, they can still be fixed afterward.

I decide I'm done for the night, anyway. Grandparents always like to get up early and they'll probably wake us up, too.

I reach to turn off my lamp but decide, just for tonight, to keep it on. It *is* a new night in a new room.

As I drift off to sleep, I hear more creaking above my head. This time, it almost sounds like footsteps.

I watch as the water ripples all around me.

This time, the pool is wider, almost like an ocean.
The water crashes around me—

I wake up, gasping for air.

I had the dream again.

The same dream I had the night I failed my swimming lesson.

This time, it was so clear. The water, the sensation of falling . . .

I'm sweating, the cool dampness already drying as the warm sunlight comes through the curtains. I don't know if it's because of my bad dream or how hot it is in this house. I'm glad I packed only shorts and tank tops if this is what I have to look forward to.

"Can we turn the air on?" I hear Capri yelling down the hall. I roll my eyes. Gosh, I'm convinced Capri has the worst attitude ever. "Does this place even *have* air-conditioning?"

"We have it, but it's sometime-y," Grandad says. "It comes on and off when it wants to. When we get too hot, we just swim in the lake or in the pool up the road."

My stomach drops again. This stupid lake everyone keeps talking about. Maybe I'll just stay in the room all day, relax on the balcony, and catch the breeze.

"Daisy! Owen! Celeste!" Grandma calls from downstairs. "Come on and get some of this breakfast!"

My stomach rumbles. Well, maybe *after* I get some of that breakfast.

There is no clock in this room, but I can tell it's early in the morning. Not as early as I'd have to get up for school, but too early for summer vacation. I walk over to the balcony door, the floor creaking under me, and open it. I step onto the balcony, the wood warm under my feet, and admire the huge oak tree in the backyard, the sunlight dancing off the leaves. And there it is, ruining my entire mood, as beautiful as it is.

The lake.

It looks innocent enough, the way the water shines in the morning sun. I love the way it looks—just like the stars I drew last night. The sun sparkles on the green-and-blue water like glitter.

But just thinking about it reminds me of my certification of participation from my swimming lessons, and I get annoyed. Mama says that I should be proud of the certificate, that it means I tried. But I still left the pool after that last lesson not knowing how to swim. Maybe I should've done what Iris suggested and told Jared right then and there how I felt that first day. Maybe he would've apologized and taught me how to swim, and I could have fun in the lake like everyone else.

"Celeste?"

I hear Grandma's voice, faintly, coming from down the stairs. I walk back in the bedroom, where my Simone Manuel poster looks like she's judging me. Mama bought it for me to inspire me to learn how to swim. Simone's such an amazing swimmer. I know she wants other Black kids to learn to swim, too. I sigh as I walk out of my room and downstairs.

I walk through the living room and see everyone already downstairs, a full breakfast spread on the table.

My stomach growls again. I see all my favorites: pancakes, eggs, grits, bacon, grapefruit. Just like Mama makes. I wonder if this is how my mom learned how to make all that good food.

Grandma looks up and smiles at me, a familiar and lazy smile like she sees me all the time. I guess that's just how grandmas are.

I realize I missed her smile, too, just like I missed Grandad's. I smile back.

"Just in time to say grace. Your grandad went to go

get something for his truck and already ate. He'll be back."

I look around the table for an empty seat. There's one by Capri. Her brown skin glistens with sweat. It looks like she's been working out. She has a bigger frown on her face than usual.

"Good morning," I say to her.

"Hey." She glances at me, then looks away.

I try again. "Uncle Howard said you'll be driving this week."

"So? I'm not going to drive you to the pool or whatever."

Her quick meanness takes me by surprise and kind of hurts my feelings. Should I be mean back? Will that make her stop? I stand up taller and say, "I don't care. I don't want to go to the pool anyway."

I don't feel like getting picked apart by her this morning. I take the empty seat in between Daisy and Grandma and across from Owen instead. Daisy is sitting up so straight that her back isn't even touching the chair.

"Good morning," I say to Daisy. She's wearing

another sundress, this time with thin, light blue stripes. My dad has a suit like this; I think the pattern is called seersucker.

"I like your dress," I tell her. This feels more natural to me, giving people compliments when I like their clothes or hair. I like being nice, not rude like Capri.

She smiles at me. "Isn't it just dreamy?"

Dreamy? That's a funny word to use to describe a dress. I don't know what to say to that, so I just smile and nod and look ahead, accidentally catching Capri's eye.

She stares at me for a second and looks back down at her untouched plate of food. Behind her head, I notice I have a direct view of the lake. It's rippling and sparkling in the sun. Way off in the distance, I see a boat. Again, I'm reminded of how I blew my swimming lessons.

I can't get away from water, I think. Not in my dreams, in the pool, or at this lake house.

Grandma grabs my hand and I grab Daisy's while Grandma blesses the food.

"Lord, we thank you for this meal. I'm thankful to spend some quality time with my grandbabies," she says. "I pray that this meal nourishes our bodies and that this is the start of a wonderful summer for us all. I hope that we all find the peace we need."

I feel a hand squeeze my shoulder and I smile. Grandad must be back from the auto shop.

"Amen," we all say in unison. I open my eyes to turn around and say hello to Grandad, but he's not there. We all drop hands, and Grandma starts passing the orange juice around the table.

"Where's Grandad?" I say, craning my head around to see the kitchen and hallway behind me.

"I told you—he's at the auto shop," Grandma says, scooping some grits onto her plate. "What's wrong?"

"I just—I just thought I felt—a hand on my shoulder." Owen looks up from his bowl of grits at me. I shake my head. "Never mind." I must have been imagining it. Owen's still watching me, and I shrug.

Owen speaks up. "Grandma, is this house haunted?" He laughs a little when he asks. "I don't like ghosts. I once watched a show where these guys explored a haunted hotel."

I know he's joking, but I think about last night when

Grandma and Daisy thought I was already downstairs when I wasn't. I was upstairs hearing giggling and voices from no one. My stomach drops a little, but I try to ignore it. I have to be imagining things.

Grandma laughs. A light titter. "Owen, you don't have anything to worry about. I pray for y'all every night. If you feel like there's an evil ghost around, just pray for God's protection and they'll go away."

Daisy nods, as if she's agreeing with her. "That's true, you know."

"You say that as if you believe in them," I say slowly. I'm not used to that. My parents would always tell me or Owen that ghosts were make-believe if we started asking too many questions after we watched a scary show or read a scary book.

Then I hear a creak.

Footsteps.

I hear them getting louder and louder and look around to see if anyone else does, too.

"Good morning to you all!" Grandad walks around the corner with a big grin. I let out a breath. I don't know who I thought was coming. He takes off his hat and wipes his bald head with the towel in his hand.

Everyone says good morning. Capri sinks down in her chair and keeps stabbing at the last piece of her pancake.

"Capri? You ready?"

Capri looks up at Grandad with narrowed, piercing eyes, but Grandad keeps smiling. If anything, his smile just softens a little bit.

The table is silent. I look from Grandad to Daisy, and then to Owen. Owen looks at me, then shrugs and looks at Capri. Daisy looks at everyone, taking it all in with her round eyes.

Capri breaks the silence by scooting her chair back so hard it scrapes the floor and bumps the window behind her. "Yes. I'll be outside."

She walks past the table, past Grandad, and according to the way the door slams, she walks outside.

I really don't understand Capri. I would've gotten in trouble for acting like that and slamming those doors at home.

Grandad only looks at the door, though, and shakes his head, his smile still calmly on his face. "We're going to test-drive the truck. I got some new parts for it this morning. I'll see you all later?" He gives Grandma a kiss on the cheek and tips his hat at the rest of us and goes outside to Capri.

"Where are they going?" Owen asked.

"Oh, just spending some quality grandfather/grand-daughter time. He wants to do that with all of you and I do, too." Grandma watches him leave and looks back at us. "I was thinking since it's so nice out, the four of us could go to the lake."

"Yes!" Owen says. He smiles but quickly hides it and looks at me.

Great. That's just what I need. I know this is a ploy to get me to get comfortable in the water. I'm not ready to swim in a lake when I can't even jump in a pool by myself.

"Listen here and listen good. These are the rules of the lake. If you break any of these rules, I won't let you go near that lake again, do you understand?"

Everyone nods, even me. Even though I'm definitely not going down with them. Grandma's warm eyes get very serious and we're all listening.

"Rule number one: Don't ever go in that lake alone, you hear me?

"Rule number two: Always wear a life jacket. We have about ten out there of all shapes and sizes and for different uses. The ones you'll probably use are the blue-and-yellow ones.

"Rule number three: Don't swim out too far, especially when it's windy. You can jump in and do small laps, but unless Grandad takes you out boating, we'll mostly be wading near the dock."

"But I can swim, Grandma. I just learned a few weeks ago," Owen says. I can feel him looking at me again, trying to see if my feelings would be hurt, but I pretend not to see him. *It's okay*, I decide. He should be proud that he passed his swimming classes.

"Oh, it's not just about that," Grandma says. "This is a lake, much different than a pool. Even the most experienced swimmers can have trouble or accidentally go out too far. I'll teach you all about that. Stay close to me in the water. You go too far and you'll have to come back inside. I mean that."

"Yes, ma'am," Daisy and Owen say.

Grandma smiles again. "Okay. Now go get your swimming things and meet me back downstairs in ten minutes. Let's have some fun!"

"Can I stay inside?" I ask. "I just want to sit on the balcony and do some drawing." It isn't entirely a lie.

Grandma nods. "Sure, baby. Whatever you want."

Relief washes over me.

"Have fun." I excuse myself from the table. I'd get out to the lake one day this week. Maybe.

I walk upstairs to my room and onto the balcony, hearing the back door slam before I close the bedroom door behind me. The sky is clear, mirroring the lake, the rays dancing off the water. I have to admit that it's beautiful.

There's a small breeze blowing. I can feel the wind blowing hot around my face. I can see it blowing through the trees. Hear it rustling through the leaves.

"Celeste . . ."

If I listen closely enough, it almost sounds like the wind is calling my name. I open my sketchbook and sit there for a while, letting the sun warm my face and studying the backyard. I can hear Owen and Grandma laugh around the lake. Even Daisy. I put my sketchbook down and watch them. They all have on life jackets. It looks like they're racing, running to the edge of the water and back. Then they jump in and splash around, not going too far out. It almost looks . . . fun. I think about grabbing my swimsuit to go down there with them, but I stop myself. How do I know that Grandma won't try to make me jump in the water like Stinky-Breath Jared did?

"Celeste."

I whip my head around.

The voice is sharp, the *T* in my name crisp, like the way a branch sounds when you step on it.

This time it *really* sounds like someone is calling me.

I don't think I'm imagining it. Even though it's hot, goose bumps form on my arms.

"Hello?" I ask. I decide to get up and see what's going on, taking Grandma's advice and saying a small prayer, just in case.

I walk into the hallway, and I don't hear anything at all. One of the bedroom doors is open. I peek into it and see a picture of a woman in a track uniform with long, pretty fingernails and a medal around her neck. The name Florence Griffith-Joyner is scrawled on the bottom. This must be the room Capri picked. If she were nicer, I'd tell her that I think it's cool that we both have Olympic medalist posters on our wall.

I realize again how quiet it is and how I heard my name but I'm upstairs.

Alone.

"Hello?" I say again.

I decide to walk downstairs.

Each stair creaks, with the third one from the top creaking the loudest. I walk downstairs and look around the living room. Nobody.

I walk into the kitchen.

I hear a giggle. A small one, like the one I heard before dinner yesterday.

I turn all the way around and see the kitchen window.

Grandma, Daisy, and Owen are still in the lake. Maybe the wind is throwing their voices this way.

There's another door open downstairs. Grandma and Grandad's bedroom. I knock on the door and walk in.

"Hello?"

I look around the room.

It looks nice and cozy, with pictures of their children and grandchildren everywhere. I see Grandma and Grandad's wedding picture and Grandma looks just like Mama in it.

Their bed looks huge, huge enough for all of us kids to pile into it.

I see another picture on their dresser. It's black and white, and faded, and it's in a white, fancy frame with all kinds of frilly designs around it. I can't make out who's in the photo, so I move closer.

I gasp and jump.

It's a picture of me.

No, no, it has to be a picture of Great-Aunt Ellie.

I pick up the picture and stare at it closely. The eyes, the nose, the mouth, even the French braids . . . it's all me. Except for her smile. It's just too sneaky.

I think about Grandma and when she told us about her at dinner. She didn't want to tell us what happened to her.

Why?

Did something bad happen?

Suddenly, I want to know a lot more about this lady who I look like.

Slowly, I reach out and touch the picture.

"Celeste?"

I jump, dropping the picture. A dark brown hand reaches around me and catches it.

I turn around.

It's Grandad.

"I didn't mean to startle you," Grandad says. "Did you need something?" I see a light coming from an open door behind him. Their bathroom. He must've been in there while I was in here . . . snooping.

I thought I heard someone call my name, and when I checked in here I got distracted by this picture of Great-Aunt Ellie because I thought it was me, I think. Even though it's the truth, it kind of sounds silly in my head. I decide not to say it.

Instead, I ask him: "Grandad? What happened to Great-Aunt Ellie? How did she die?"

Grandad takes a deep breath, and it takes a long time for him to let it back out. "You have to ask your grandmother that."

"I did, yesterday, but she wouldn't tell us. She said, 'We shouldn't talk about that right now.'"

"I have to agree with her, Celeste," he says. "Maybe . . . a little later."

I wonder if he means later on today or later this week, but I don't ask. I just nod and say okay.

I wonder what happened to Great-Aunt Ellie, and why Grandma and Grandad are keeping it such a secret.

CHAPTER 3

I walk back upstairs and realize Capri's door is shut, and I hear someone walking around on the other side. If Grandad was already in his bathroom when I went in his room, Capri could have already been upstairs. Hmm. I bet she was the one calling my name and trying to scare me. I just shake my head and walk back into my room and onto the balcony.

It's almost lunchtime. I hear the back door burst open as everyone comes back from the lake and walks up to their rooms to change out of their wet suits.

Owen comes onto the balcony and tells me how cool the lake water is. I don't want to feel jealous. I feel happy for my brother. I wish I felt the same way he does. But every time I think about swimming, I think about failing my swimming lessons and feel ashamed.

I want to tell him about hearing someone call my name, but I don't want him to get scared and start looking up facts about haunted lake houses to tell everyone at dinner. My brother can't help himself once he gets started.

After I draw for a while, I smell food, and decide to go downstairs. Everyone is already sitting there except for Grandad and Capri. They're all laughing about something funny Owen did in the water. Grandma tells us we're going to wait for Capri to come downstairs before we start eating.

After a little while, right when my stomach starts to growl, I hear stomping.

"Hey, Capri—" we all fix our mouths to say, but Capri doesn't even stop at the table. She stomps past, not saying anything to anyone, pours a glass of water, and goes back upstairs, slamming her door.

I've had enough. We all waited for Capri and Grandad to come back before we started eating lunch, and she goes upstairs without saying anything to us? That's it. If she gets an attitude with me again, I'm going to build up the courage to ask her what her problem is. If all she's going to do is stomp around and be mean, why doesn't she just go home?

"Is something wrong?" Owen asks, breaking the silence that was starting to form around the table.

Grandad sighs as he sits down, but he still has a smile on his face. I realize he's a very patient person. "Nothing's wrong. We just had a good ol' drive around town, that's all."

Owen and I exchange a puzzled look. I shrug my shoulders at him. I decide I'm not going to try to figure Capri out anymore. I'm just ready to eat my lunch.

"You should talk to your cousin," Grandma says. "Cousins are some of your first best friends. You should be there for each other."

I don't know about all of that. I already have my best friends back at school, and Owen.

"Now let's eat and let some of this good food clear the air," Grandad says, looking toward the stairwell. "She'll be down soon, don't you worry. Nobody can resist your grandma's cooking."

He sits down and we close our eyes and say grace. Sure enough, when I open my eyes, Capri is sitting right in front of me. I didn't even hear her coming down the stairs.

Later, everyone is doing their own thing. Owen is taking a walk around the neighborhood with Grandad. Daisy is blaring Ella Fitzgerald, the legendary jazz singer, through the portable record player she brought with her. Grandma is humming and singing along with the music. I'm not sure what Capri is doing, but I think she went for a jog. I didn't bother to ask.

It's sunny out, so I decide to walk in the backyard with my pad and pencils and get a closer view of the lake.

I slip out the back door and walk down the wooden steps. I see the deck, the big oak tree, and freshly cut grass all around. This would be the perfect place to lay a blanket out and eat lunch. I wonder if Grandma and Grandad ever do that.

There's a bench closer to the lake—but not too close—so I walk toward it. The farther I get from the house, the quieter it seems. I feel a chill on the back of my neck, despite how hot it is.

I sit down and start to sketch the lake. I can see the ripples in the water and the ducks floating on top more closely. I smile as I sketch them.

I whip my head around. I have the feeling that someone is standing behind me, but I don't see anyone. That's odd. I keep sketching.

I stare at the lake. It goes as far as I can see, meeting the sky in the distance.

Have I seen this view before? It looks so familiar. Maybe in photographs?

A warm breeze blows and I shiver. Again, I feel like someone is standing behind me and I whip my head around. I don't see anything except the sunlight reflecting off the attic window.

It's shining so bright, almost like a light is on up there.

Is a light on up there?

It flickers off. Then on, then off again.

"Celeste. Celeste. Celeste."

The light is turning on and off to the same rhythm I'm hearing my name. I turn back around, facing the lake again. Of course, nobody is there.

Who said that?

I watch the small breeze blow through the lake and sit back down. Someone taps me on my shoulder.

I scream and jump back up.

"I'm sorry! I didn't mean to scare you!" Owen says.

"Oh! It's just you. I thought I heard someone calling my name."

"I didn't call your name," Owen says.

"You didn't?" I ask. "Then—"

It's probably just the wind again, Celeste, I think.

But I'm not so sure.

"Owen, did you see a light in the attic? Is Grandad upstairs?"

"No, I don't think so. After we came back from our walk, Grandad went to his room."

Maybe I need to tell Grandma and Grandad something is wrong with the light in their attic. "How was your walk with Grandad?" I ask, trying to keep my mind off the attic and my name on the wind.

"It was great! Except for the fact that he tried to get me to go on a walking trail in those woods." He points to the group of trees at the edge of the backyard. "But it's okay, he doesn't know that I don't do mountain lions."

"Owen. I doubt that there are mountain lions anywhere around here."

The sunlight sparkles on the attic again, catching my attention.

"I really thought I saw a light up there. Are you sure no one is upstairs?"

"Everyone's downstairs now. Oh, except for Capri. I heard her in her room."

Capri. It's starting to make sense. I'll bet she was the one calling my name yesterday and the one playing in the attic today because she knows I'm outside!

"I bet she's in the attic, trying to scare me," I tell Owen.

"You think she'd try to scare you?" Owen asks. "Why?"

"She's been mean to me as soon as we got here," I say.

"Yeah, she has been in a pretty bad mood." Owen shrugs. "Teenagers. Anyway, can I see your drawing?"

I show Owen the drawing that I came up with out here. Just a view of the lake, the sunlight, and the ducks.

"This is great," he says. "Does this mean you'll get in the lake this week?"

I sigh. "I don't know, Owen. I just don't care anymore after my last swimming lesson, and now I've been having a weird dream about falling in water." Owen is the first person I've told about my nightmare. "It makes me not want to learn anymore. At least until that nightmare goes away."

"Or maybe you have it backward," Owen says. "Maybe your dream will go away the more you get into the water."

Hmm. I didn't think of that. "Maybe you're right" is all I say.

"Celeste!"

My heart thumps.

"Owen!"

We turn around and see Grandma standing at the back door. Maybe *she* was the one who called my name earlier.

"Yes, ma'am?" we answer back.

"Y'all aren't in that lake water, are you?"

"Nope! Celeste is just drawing." Owen points to my sketch pad.

Grandma smiles. "Oh, okay. Just checking on you."

She closes the screen door but leaves the actual door open, probably to let some air in.

"Let's go inside," I say. Owen and I walk back to the house. But I can't help but notice the sunlight shining on the attic again, and the feeling that someone is right behind me, about to call my name.

CHAPTER 4

I run upstairs to try and take a quick shower before dinner. When I reach the top step, Capri turns the corner from her room and runs smack into me.

"Ouch!" we both yell.

"Watch where you're going!" she says.

I stand up straighter. "I was already on the stairs. Did you hear me coming?"

"Just move," she says, shoving me a little. I remember my promise to myself, to say something if she continues to be mean.

"You don't have to be so rude all the time," I say. "You could say excuse me or sorry."

She turns around on the steps. I'm realizing how tall she is. But since I'm at the top of the stairs, it feels like we're the same height.

Kind of.

"Sorry," she says, smirking a little. But I can tell she doesn't mean it.

"I didn't do anything for you to be so mean," I keep going. "And—and if you're trying to scare me. Stop."

I can tell this catches her off guard, unless she's a good actress. "Scare you? How am I trying to scare you?"

"You know what you did! I heard somebody calling my name outside today and yesterday—you were the only one upstairs. And later you turned the light on and off in the attic to try and scare me."

As if on cue, the attic light above me flickers on and off.

We both look at it and at each other, not sure of what to say.

"Well, now you know that wasn't me, huh?" she says. "This house is old. That light is probably just messed up. I have better things to do than prank you."

Like what? I want to ask her.

"But were you calling my name?" I continue. "Saying 'Celeste' in a scary way over and over again?"

She sighs. "What do you think?" she says, and she turns around and goes downstairs.

I think you were, I want to say, but I just don't.

Maybe there's a better way to handle this.

I go to my bedroom to get my pajamas for after my shower, and I look up at the attic again.

I really need to tell Grandad to look at that.

It flickers again, but this time it stays on.

———

While I'm in the shower, I'm thinking about how both Jared and Capri were mean to me. Because I let Jared be mean to me, I didn't learn how to swim. I can't let Capri be mean to me, too.

Since she pranked me, I'm going to prank her back. That will show her to leave me alone.

I'm not like her or Iris. I can't come up with quick comebacks in time, so this is the next best thing.

I try to make myself like what I'm doing. I smile at myself in the mirror, but I don't even look like myself. The sneakiness of it makes me look like Great-Aunt Ellie.

I can hear Capri still downstairs, so I go hide in her closet. Her closet is perfectly neat and organized by color. All her sneakers and sandals are lined up like they would be in a shoe store. It's so neat, it's hard to find a place to hide, but I push myself way in the back of the closet, behind her clothes and bags.

It feels like I'm waiting forever until I finally hear her come into her room.

I whisper as softly as I can.

"Capri."

I still hear her rummaging around her room, her bracelets dangling.

She must not have heard me. I whisper a little louder.

"Capri."

I try to make my voice sound shaky and scary.

Her footsteps stop.

"Who said that?"

I hold my mouth to keep from giggling, but no giggle comes anyway. She kind of sounds scared. I feel bad, but I try to talk myself out of it. Did she feel bad when she was mean to me or trying to prank me? No.

I'm waiting for her to run downstairs so I can run back in my room and pretend I'm taking a nap.

It's still silent. I picture her looking around.

"Capri," I whisper even louder.

Maybe now she'll—

Suddenly, I'm blinded by light as the door opens.

"Who's in here?" she yells.

I try to stay still. *Wow, she's brave*, I think. If I thought a noise was coming from my closet, I definitely wouldn't open the door.

I stay still, hoping she'll go away. My stomach drops as she picks up the bag I'm hiding behind.

"Celeste! What do you think you're doing?" she yells.

She's yelling so loudly that I hear a bunch of other footsteps come upstairs.

"What's going on?" I hear a voice. Grandma.

Oh no.

"Celeste was in my closet calling my name and trying to scare me!"

I sigh as I stand up and walk out of the closet. Not only is Grandma here, but I see Owen and

Daisy in the hallway and Grandad is coming upstairs.

"Celeste? What are you doing?" Grandma asks.

"I told you," Capri says, but her voice gets really soft with Grandma.

I decide to tell the truth. "Capri has been pranking me, so I decided to prank her back."

"I told you I didn't do that," Capri says, her voice getting loud and mean again.

"You didn't. You just told me you weren't playing with the attic light."

"The attic light?" Grandad says. "That attic light has been broken for years."

"It has?" Capri and I say in unison.

"But I saw it on," I say. I wait for Capri to say "me too," but she doesn't.

"Oh, Celeste, you should apologize to your cousin for trying to scare her," Grandma says. "Cousins need to stick together, not scare each other."

That's not fair, I think. She needs to apologize for being mean to me!

I think about the way Capri apologized earlier. With

a smirk. I try to do the same thing. "Sorry," I say, just like her. I know she gets it, because she narrows her eyes.

"Celeste, that wasn't meaningful," Grandma says.

It wasn't meaningful when she did it, either! I want to scream. I want to tell them how mean Capri has been being to me, but now I feel like a baby. And embarrassed.

I sigh. "I'm sorry," I say. I do feel bad. But I wish Capri would mean it, too.

"It's okay," Capri says.

"Well, all's well that ends well," Grandad says. "Let's go downstairs and start dinner, shall we?" He smiles at us and I try to smile back.

Capri, Daisy, and Grandma follow Grandad while Owen stays behind. "Celeste, are you okay? You've never pranked anyone before. Have you?"

"No. I know," I say. "I was just tired of her being mean to me."

"It's okay," he says. "Just try to ignore her. Maybe she's mad about something else."

Maybe, but it seems like she's taking it out on me.

I follow Owen downstairs and see the attic light flicker again. Wait, didn't Grandad say it was broken? I have to show him that it's flickering. He must've made a mistake when he said that.

Right?

CHAPTER 5

After I went to bed last night, I stayed awake still feeling embarrassed and a little ashamed about what I did. But this morning, I want to start fresh.

I'm just not going to speak to Capri. I'm only going to talk to Grandma, Grandad, Daisy, and Owen.

When I walk downstairs for breakfast, I see the light in the attic flicker on and off, and it reminds me to tell Grandad about it. When I get to the bottom step, Grandad is coming through the door. He's always doing something. I wonder if he ever just sits down and watches TV sometimes.

"Good morning, Celeste," he says. "Feeling good?"

I wonder if he knows I felt bad about last night. I nod my head.

"Grandad, I wanted to tell you, but I think you made

a mistake about the attic light. I saw it turn on and off a few times last night."

He raises his eyebrow. "Oh? Are you sure? From what I can remember, the switch stopped working, so I took the whole thing apart."

"Really?" I say. That can't be right.

"I'm almost sure of it. Let's check it out."

I follow Grandad back upstairs and watch as he reaches up and pulls the string to let the attic door down. He unfolds the attic steps and walks up. He turns around and looks at me. "Helloooo down there!" he says, making his voice echo. I giggle.

"You want to come up?"

"Sure." I steady myself on the steps and walk up behind him. It's dark. I wait for him to turn on the light, but he doesn't.

"See? This was the only light switch up here," he says. He points to a rectangular hole in the wall.

"And look, there's not even a light bulb screwed in." He points above us, and sure enough, it's empty.

This gives me a funny feeling in my stomach. I may have imagined someone saying my name, but I know for sure I saw a bright light up here. Capri said twice that she didn't try to prank me by flashing a light up here. Was she telling the truth?

I start to tell myself I imagined that, too, but I know what I saw.

"But I saw it, Grandad," I say. "It was big and bright. I saw it yesterday in the hallway, while I was down at the lake, and—"

Then I remember. I saw it the first day we got here.

Capri was standing right beside me. If it wasn't her, then . . .

Who?

"You really saw a light up here, huh?" Grandad says. He starts to look around the attic. "We haven't been up here in at least a year."

Grandad walks around the attic and looks around, his eyebrows scrunched together like he's concentrating really hard. It makes me feel good that he believes me.

"I really did, Grandad," I say. I'm waiting for a light to turn on once Grandad finds it, but it never does.

I follow him to the edge of the attic, to the window,

and look down and see the lake. I can see where I was sitting and drawing.

Grandad turns to look at me.

"I'm sorry, darling, but I really don't know what it could've been," he says. I just nod. It's not that he doesn't believe me, but he doesn't know where a light could come from. I don't, either.

A chill runs down my back. If there's no working light in here, what does that mean?

My eyes catch on a box right below the window. It looks like it was taped up before, but the tape is slightly ripped at the top.

I see a pair of eyes looking back at me.

I gasp, but then I realize the eyes are coming from a photo that shows through the gap in the box.

"What's in here?" I ask. I open the box a little more, but Grandad gently grabs my hand and closes the box.

"Celeste, I'm sorry, but I don't think Grandma would want you to see that," he says.

"Why?" I ask.

Grandad looks at me. I can tell he's torn about what to say.

"It's something you'll have to talk to her about," he says. "This box is full of things about your great-aunt Ellie."

But I already tried that, and she already told me, Not now, I think.

Is Grandma hiding something about Great-Aunt Ellie?

"Come on, let's go downstairs for breakfast," Grandad says.

I just nod and walk with him. The attic is still dark, but I have the feeling I'm being watched. I turn around and realize the box is open again, this time all the way. I still see the pair of eyes peeking out.

"Gr—" I try to tell Grandad, but my voice is stuck in my throat.

Between the attic light and the secrets Grandma's hiding, I'm starting to feel a little nervous at this lake house.

It's nighttime now and I still feel uneasy. I wonder if that box is open, those eyes still peeking all around. I wonder if the attic light is flickering on and off, on and off, even though there's no light bulb. Is it on now? Twice, I've cracked open my door to check, to look up at the ceiling and see if any light seeps through the cracks of the attic door. This time, I decide I'll tell Grandad if I see it. But it hasn't come on.

At dinner, I did a great job of ignoring Capri, but it was hard. I could tell she noticed, because she kept looking at me out of the corner of her eye. But I don't want to be friends with someone mean.

And what was in that box that Grandma doesn't want us to see so badly? Did something so terrible happen to Great-Aunt Ellie that she doesn't want us to know? Did—did Grandma do something to her?

I shake the thought out of my head. No way. Grandma loved Great-Aunt Ellie. She could never—

"Aah!"

A loud scream fills my ears.

My heart thumps, and the hairs stand up on my arms.

What's going on?

I hear the scream again and jump out of bed.

"Help! Leave me alone!"

It's Owen.

CHAPTER 6

"Owen?"

I run to his room, the floorboards creaking under my feet.

"Owen!"

My hands are so slippery when I turn the knob.

"Owen? Are you okay?"

"Celeste, stop! You're scaring me!"

I push open the door and I see my brother. His eyes are wide and he's curled up at the edge of the bed.

I hear a big BOOM from inside the closet that makes me jump back.

"Celeste, please . . . leave me alone . . ."

"Owen!"

He sees my face and screams again.

"Owen! Stop! It's me! Calm down, okay?"

"No . . ."

I run to the closet door and open it, not sure about what I'm going to find. It reminds me of hiding in Capri's closet earlier. I said I'd never open a closet door if I felt afraid of what was behind it, but I'm doing it now.

Nothing.

I reach over and turn on the closet light, my heart pounding as I push back the clothes.

Now the silence is ringing in my ears. There was a big boom; I know I heard it!

I turn around to look at Owen and he looks away from me.

"Owen?"

I walk over to him and he tries to run. I grab his shoulders and force him to look at me.

"It's me! Celeste. Your sister. What's going on in here? What was the noise?"

His breathing slows down. He takes a deep breath.

"Celeste, why would you try to prank *me*? That was really mean."

For a second, I don't know what to say. "Prank you? I wasn't—"

"Celeste, please," Owen says. He's still shivering. "I saw you. I saw you after that big boom from my closet woke me up. You were standing in the closet just staring at me with a scary look on your face and not saying anything. And—and you were making my hiking boots look like they were . . . floating toward me. They slammed into the wall behind me and almost hit me. You almost hurt me, Celeste."

"What?" I ask Owen, shaking my head. "Are you sure you weren't dreaming?"

"We both know I wasn't dreaming, Celeste," he says. He points a shaking finger to the wall behind his bed. "Look."

We both look and see muddy footprints tracked across the wall. They are all different sizes, like the boots hit the wall a lot of times, a lot of different ways. I gasp.

"Oh my gosh! Who did that?" I ask him. He just looks at me for a second and shakes his head . . . like he's disappointed in me.

"Oh, Owen." I hug him as I hear footsteps come into the bedroom. Daisy and Capri.

"What's going on in here?" Capri says.

"Owen, are you okay?" Daisy asks.

Owen looks at me and then Daisy and Capri, but he doesn't say anything.

"It's . . . nothing," he says.

Daisy and Capri look at him, confused. They're walking toward us when I notice movement out of the corner of my eye, some type of flicker coming from the closet.

"Look!" I yell. "Did y'all see that?" I point to the closet and they turn, following my finger.

SLAM!

I jump as a noise turns our attention back to the wall. I see Owen's hiking boots tumble to the ground beside me. It looks like there are more footprints on the wall than there were just a second ago.

Way more. How could that have happened so fast?

Everyone looks back at me, like I made the noise.

I leap up and point at the shoes. "The shoes! They—they moved by themselves!"

"Celeste . . ." Owen says. He looks tired and strained.

"You—" Daisy stops and shrugs. "I think the shoes must have just fallen over."

Capri walks over to put them back upright, like nothing happened.

"Fell *over*? Something just moved in the closet," I say, walking to the closet door and pulling it wide open again. "And then the shoes rose by *themselves* and hit the wall!"

Didn't they?

Now everyone's attention is back on the wall and the footprints. Owen still doesn't say anything.

Capri looks at the wall, the shoes, the closet, Owen, and then me. Her eyes narrow. "Celeste, were you trying to prank Owen now, too?"

"No!" I say. "Why would I prank my own brother?"

"Well, you pranked me," Capri says back.

"No, I—" Then I stop. I did prank her. "But only because you pranked me first."

"No, I didn't! How many times do I have to tell you that?"

"Well, I thought you did! But Owen didn't do anything to me at all!"

Meanwhile, Owen is still shivering, looking at me.

I turn to my brother. "Owen, you believe me, don't you?"

We look at each other for a long second while I wait for him to say yes, but he doesn't say anything.

"Owen?" I ask again.

"Celeste, I—I saw you," he says. He looks at Daisy and Capri. "Please, don't tell Grandma and Grandad. It's okay. It was just a joke."

"But Owen, I didn't do anything!" I start to yell, and I feel tears stinging the corners of my eyes. Why don't they believe me? "I was just lying in bed until I heard Owen! I didn't even come out of my room!"

Daisy looks at me, her eyes so round in the dim hallway light that they remind me of owl eyes. "Celeste, I did hear your room door open."

"Well, I *did* open the door, but I was checking to see if the attic light was still on." I'm telling the truth, but I know that it sounds strange to them.

"I thought you said Grandad said there's no attic light?" Owen finally says.

"I know that, but I saw it. Capri, you saw it, too!" I say.

Capri's eyes widen, but she doesn't say anything.

"It's okay, everyone, really. I'm fine," Owen says. "Let's just drop it."

"Okay, good night," Daisy says. Capri looks at me for a second like she wants to say something, then walks behind Daisy out of the room.

Owen and I are in his room for a second, silent. Finally, he turns to me.

"Celeste, are you okay?" he says. "You aren't acting like yourself."

"Owen, you have to believe me. I would never prank you like that! How would I even get into your closet without you knowing? Or make the hiking shoes *float* without you seeing me?" I ask.

"I—I don't know," Owen says, his eyebrows knitting together. "Maybe with—with some type of string. It was dark, so it's easy to hide yourself."

I can't believe what I'm hearing.

"I want to believe you, Celeste, but I saw you with my own eyes."

I put my face in my hands and let the tears fall down. When I look back up, Owen is looking at me, concerned.

"It's okay, let's just get some sleep and start fresh in the morning." He pats my back, turns off the light, and lies back down. He even turns over while I'm still in the room and faces the dirty wall. Maybe it's the darkness, but it looks like the footprints are already fading.

I think he's upset with me, but I know my brother, he'll be over it by the morning. But I'm still upset that he thinks I did it.

I walk to my room and get back in my own bed. I can't fall asleep, because I keep thinking about how my cousins and brother don't believe me.

But if I didn't go into Owen's room and prank him, who did?

CHAPTER 7

The next morning, the sky is gray and it matches my mood. I couldn't sleep because I had that same dream again where I'm falling into a big body of water, and I kept thinking about what happened with Owen last night. To make matters worse, during breakfast, Grandad asked if I would like to go to the pool with him.

I'm hoping it rains before we even get in the car so Grandad can cancel the trip, but it doesn't. At least we aren't starting off in the lake.

"I would never put you in that lake to teach you how to swim," Grandad says when I tell him this. "Maybe that'll be the next step, after you are more comfortable. Safety above all. I was a lifeguard, you know."

I nod. Even though I'm still nervous, a weight is lifted off my shoulders at the idea that I won't be thrown into that endless lake.

I get in his rusty blue pickup truck. It's a two-seater.

Grandad picks up on my mood and asks me what's wrong.

I start to say "Nothing," but Grandad is easy to talk to, like Dad. Mom says Dad reminds her of Grandad, and I bet this is why.

"Grandad?" I ask. "How can you get people to listen to you?"

I think about Stinky-Breath Jared calling me the wrong name, Capri yelling at me, and Owen not believing me. The last one hurts. Owen always believes me.

"Listen to you?" Grandad says. "Well, it's so many ways. Some people are loud and talk a lot, some people are quiet and say a few powerful words. Some people sing or write speeches. You have to figure out what works for you."

I think about this. I don't think I'm a good singer, and I don't like being mean. I'm not very loud. I like drawing and giving people compliments and telling the truth, even when people don't believe me. But is that enough? I ask Grandad this.

"It'll always be enough for the right people at the right time," Grandad says. He reaches over and squeezes my shoulder.

I sure hope so.

We pull up to what looks like another side of the lake. When we get out of the car and get closer to it, though, I see there's a small building in front of the lake that looks like a clubhouse. Beyond it is a small pool. There are about four people in it right now, and a few people off to the side in chairs, relaxing and reading magazines.

"We're going to start in here," Grandad says. "No pressure. Just get in the water and wade a little bit."

Grandad takes out a key and uses it to open the gate that leads to the pool. When he swings the door open, it squeaks really loudly. Everyone looks up, I guess because of the noise. A little girl with bright red, curly hair and freckles walks up to me.

"This would look really pretty in your hair." She holds out her hand, revealing a small white flower. "My name is Sarah."

I smile at her. "Hi, Sarah," I say. I take the flower from her. "Thank you. It's really nice."

Sarah waves and runs and jumps in the pool, then swims to a woman who looks like she's Mama's age. She does this without a second thought, like the strawberry toddler I saw at my swimming lessons. I wonder when she learned how to swim and whether it was hard for her.

When Grandad and I keep walking, the woman Sarah swam to is still looking at us. I look at her, trying to catch her eye, and she looks away.

"What is she staring at?" I whisper to Grandad. I wonder if she can tell I can't swim. Is it that obvious?

"Now, don't you worry about that," Grandad says. "Come on, let's get in the pool."

I appreciate that Grandad doesn't stand at the deep end of the pool and force me to jump into his arms. We walk over to the three-foot side. I'm almost five feet, so it's not covering me too much. Grandad gets in beside me. I feel safe with him so close. I begin to relax a little.

"Just get comfortable with the water. I'm right here and I won't let you out of my sight," says Grandad.

I run my arms under the water, watching the ripples. The water is extra cold today, since there's barely any sun out, but my body gradually gets used to it. I stand on my tippy-toes and spin, the water sloshing around me. I catch the eye of the woman still looking at Grandad and me. I try to ignore her and focus on the water. It's not so bad, especially since we are by the steps and I can feel my toes hit the floor.

I do this a little while longer until I see the woman coming closer to me and Grandad.

"Grandad," I say, pointing at her. He turns his head. She doesn't look happy.

"This pool is only for lake homeowners," she says.

"Yes, I know. I am a lake homeowner," Grandad says. He smiles a little at the lady and turns back around toward me. The lady doesn't move.

"I'd like to see proof," she says after a few minutes of watching me twirl around the pool.

"Oh, Grandad has a key," I tell her. "Do you work here?"

She narrows her eyes at me.

Maybe she didn't hear me, I think.

"Do you work here?" I ask her again. "Grandad has a key, don't you, Grandad?"

"No, I don't work here," the lady says.

"And that's exactly why I don't have to prove anything to you," Grandad says. "I have a right to be here, just like you do."

"I don't believe that you live here," the lady says. I look past her at Sarah, still swimming in the water. I can't believe she left her child unattended to bother Grandad. I wonder if Grandad will just show her his key so she will leave us alone. If he shows her his key, she'll believe us. But why doesn't she believe us already?

"Maybe I don't believe you live here," Grandad says. "What if I said, 'Show me *your* key'? I've been living here probably since before you were born. Miss, I'm just trying to swim with my granddaughter. In the community I live in."

The lady scoffs.

It hits me like a wave. I know exactly what's going on. I take a deep, shaky breath.

"Did you ask these other people if they live here?" I gesture to the people around us, still in their chairs and reading their magazines. Some of them start to look up. "Or did you only come to ask my grandad because he is a Black man? He was a lifeguard, you know. He built his lake house with his bare hands. Swimming is very important to our family!"

"We don't have to explain anything to her, Celeste," Grandad says. "It's not worth it."

"You and your granddaughter don't have to make a scene," the lady says. "Or get all loud. I was just asking if he was trespassing."

Loud? We aren't even yelling.

I take a deep breath. All I have to do is tell the truth.

"We aren't making a scene, we are answering your question," I say. "Ma'am, I think you are being racist. And racism is stupid." If I were at home, I'd get in trouble for saying *stupid*, but Grandad doesn't say anything.

"For goodness' sake, just leave them alone. That's Mr. Hawthorne. I see him around here every summer." A man who looks around my dad's age sits up off his pool chair and says this. I thought he was sleeping.

"Well, then." The lady leaves us alone and goes back to the other end of the pool, where she yells at Sarah for trying to swim to the deep end of the pool. Sarah wouldn't have had the chance to do that behind her back if she just would've minded her business.

"She didn't even apologize," I say to Grandad, who waves a thank-you at the man who spoke up. The man smiles at Grandad, shakes his head at the lady, and closes his eyes again. It's not fair. She might not even have believed us if he hadn't spoken up. What if she would've tried to call the police on us?

Suddenly, I want to get out of the pool. My stomach flips the same way it did when I saw the light in the attic, heard my name in the wind. What was the point of swimming if people don't even want us in the pool? I ask Grandad this.

"That's exactly why we should learn," Grandad said. "It's our right. With every second we're in the pool, we're doing something that our ancestors weren't allowed to do."

I think about Simone Manuel. I bet they'd be *super* proud of her.

I decide to stay in the pool, but I feel a drop fall on my forehead. At first, I think it's a little girl wading beside us, who splashes us by accident and then apologizes, but then I realize it's drizzling.

"It looks like the sky is about to open up," Grandad says. "Come on, let's go home and eat some fresh fish."

Grandad and I get out of the pool and he wraps my towel around my shoulders. We walk to the gate and Sarah comes and stands in front of the gate, blocking it.

Grandad and I look at each other. Is she going to be mean now because of what happened with her mom? If she told her daughter about us, what did she even say?

Sarah waves at us, her red hair dark and slick from the water.

"I hope you come back tomorrow," she says.

CHAPTER 8

When Grandad and I walk in the door, the smell of fried fish fills the air. It reminds me of being at home, where Mama and I slather our fish with hot sauce, Owen loads his with tartar sauce, and Dad puts his between two pieces of white bread that are covered with mustard. The first time I saw him do this, I laughed. "It reminds me of being a kid," he said. He let me taste a bite.

Grandma has mustard, tartar sauce, and hot sauce on the table with the fish, along with some white rice and tomatoes. At home, we eat the tomatoes on top of the white rice whenever we have fish. I realize Mama uses all of Grandma's recipes.

"How was it?" Capri mutters to me, passing me the hot sauce after we sit down and say grace. I'm surprised that she's speaking to me without being mean.

"It was okay. I got in the water. I even swam a little bit. There was a woman there bothering Grandad. She said that she needed to see proof that he lived there."

"Who?" Grandma says, taking her seat beside me. "Jim, who said that?"

Grandad waves a hand. "Nothing to worry about. Just a woman stuck in her bad ways."

"I hate when people don't mind their business," Capri says, sucking her teeth. "Dang. All y'all were trying to do is have some fun at the pool. If I was there, I would've told her about herself."

She would've stuck up for us? Wow.

"There was no need for that," Grandad says. "Plus, Celeste told her some things she probably needed to hear. I bet she'll go to sleep tonight thinking about what you said."

I smile a little. Maybe Grandad is right.

"I'm proud of you, Celeste," Owen says, grinning up at me and dipping his piece of fish into tartar sauce. "For both things."

"Thanks," I say. I'm glad my brother feels better, but I still hate that he thinks I pranked him.

"Oh, Celeste, you're too young to concern yourself with people like that," Grandma says. She looks at Grandad, a worried expression on her face. "Imagine having to tell a grown woman what's right at that age."

Grandma looks lost in thought for a second, then her eyes meet mine. She sighs and says, "Not only do you look like Ellie, you act like her, too."

"I don't think so, Grandma," I say. "It seems like she was more mischievous."

I try to look straight at Grandma when I say this, because I'm sure everyone at the table thinks I'm lying. But I know that I only pranked someone once and didn't like it.

"She could be. But you spoke up when something was wrong and that's important," Grandma says. She touches my hand and looks me in the eye. "Just don't go showing out about it like she did."

"How did she show out?" I ask. Grandma's smile fades a little and she looks away.

"Don't worry about it, baby" is all she says. My

stomach drops. Grandma still doesn't want to tell me more about Great-Aunt Ellie. I think about the box in the attic, hiding her secrets.

I try a different approach. "Can you tell me what she was like?"

Grandma takes a sip of her water and looks at me. "She loved to laugh. She was a prankster. She loved to play pranks on me, on our parents, on anyone she could. She didn't take mess from anyone. If you disrespected her, I felt sorry for you." Grandma laughs, but there's a sadness to her voice.

"I bet you loved her a lot, didn't you?" Daisy asks.

"Still do and always will," Grandma says. "Nothing will change that."

"What was her favorite color?" Daisy asks. "Mine is yellow."

"Ellie's favorite color was green. Everything she owned was green. I remember my mom used to say that was the only reason she could get her to eat her vegetables." Grandma laughs again.

I hear a boom off in the distance, and lightning flashes across the sky, lighting up the lake in front of me.

"Ooh-*wee*," Grandad says. "It's about to pour down. I'm going to sit outside and watch the storm for a little while. Anyone care to join me?"

"Why?" asks Capri.

Grandad shrugs, wiping his mouth on a napkin. "I've always loved nature. I feel so at peace, even when a storm is raging."

Owen and I exchange a glance, both agreeing with our eyes that we'd sit outside and watch the storm with Grandad. We'd never get to do that at home. Dad always thinks we should turn everything off and close all the windows during a storm.

"Sure, after I finish eating," Capri says. She looks at me and hesitates. I take a deep breath, just in case she says something mean. I want to be ready to say something back, even if I don't say it back in a mean way.

"Celeste, some of your braids have gotten fuzzy from the pool," she says.

I *knew* she'd say something mean. I open my mouth to say something back. "I—"

"Let me redo them for you while we sit outside."

I stretch my eyes. "Really?"

She shrugs. "Sure. They have to last the whole week. I'm good at braiding hair. I did my own."

She touches her braids when she says this. They look great, so even and perfect.

"Thank you," I say.

Grandma looks at all of us and smiles again. But Daisy's eyes are stretched wide and she's stopped eating.

"Daisy, is something wrong?" Grandma asks.

She looks at Grandma and shakes her head, but when the thunder comes again, she almost jumps out of her seat.

"It's nothing to be afraid of," Grandad says. "It's just pressure in the air."

"Our house could blow away," Daisy says. "It could be a tornado."

"Well, now. I don't think this is a—" Grandad starts.

"The lights could go out," Daisy says, a whimper in her voice. "A lightning bolt could strike the house and set it on fire!"

The next boom of thunder shakes the entire house.

We hear heavier pitter-patter on the ceiling. It's coming down so hard, I can't tell if it's heavy rain or hail.

"See!" Daisy yells. Well, it's not really loud, but it is for Daisy.

"Come here, sweetie," Grandma says, her arms spread wide. Daisy hesitates for a second, but then she gets up and sits in Grandma's lap. Grandma rubs Daisy's forehead. No one can resist a hug from Grandma.

Grandad looks around the table. "My grandkids. All of you are afraid of something. Do you know that?"

"Not me," Owen says, eating a forkful of rice.

"Not true," I say. "When Grandad wanted to hike the trail with you, you completely said no."

"Oh, that's not a fear," Owen says. "That's just logical. I just watched a documentary on hiking trails and they can be dangerous. What if there are mountain lions? We have to be safe."

"There are no mountain lions—" Grandad shakes his head. "Well, this week is as good a time as any to conquer these fears. You kids wouldn't believe the things I've seen in my day. And I'm still here."

The thunder booms and Daisy whimpers again. I feel sorry for her. I can avoid pools, but you can't always avoid rain.

Capri and I beat Grandad and Owen outside. Daisy was afraid to come outside, so she and Grandma are sitting in the living room.

Capri brings a small bag with all her tools: a comb, a brush, a smaller brush, a spray bottle of water, a scarf, and gel. She unravels my braids and my scalp feels free and relaxed. She rubs my scalp with her fingers and starts detangling my hair.

The thunder is getting farther away, but the rain is steady. I close my eyes for a second and let myself relax.

Once she parts my hair, I take a deep breath and ask Capri what I've been wanting to ask her since she got here.

"Capri?" I ask.

"Huh? Am I pulling your hair too tight?"

"No, it's not that. It's just . . . why are you so mean to me?"

She stops braiding and leans over my shoulder to look at me. "Do you really think I'm mean to you?"

I start to take it back, but I want to tell the truth. "Yes," I say.

Capri sighs and braids my hair for a second. Thunder rumbles softly. She puts gel on my scalp and it feels cool, like the air outside now that it's raining. I think that she's not going to say anything else, so I keep going. "When we first got here, you rolled your eyes when we were talking to your dad. You told me that you wouldn't drive me to the pool. And you were mean to me on the steps that day—"

"I'm sorry," she says.

"Really?"

"Yeah. I just have a lot going on. I want to go to the Olympics one day and the only thing on my mind is running track. So I'm trying to make straight As and run when I can. But Mama and Daddy said I need to take a break and enjoy my summer. And when the school year starts, they won't be able to pick me up from practice anymore, so I have to—to—"

She takes a breath and braids again for a while.

"I have to get my driver's license. But I failed the test already." She says this last part softly.

"You failed the test?" I ask.

"Yeah. And I don't like failure. But I think I took the test before I was ready. And now I'm afraid I'll fail again. I don't like making mistakes."

"That's just like me in my swimming lesson. I failed that, too."

"You can't fail a swimming lesson. You don't need a swimming license for that kind of swimming," she says, and we laugh. "But I get it. Were you afraid?"

"No. I just hated my instructor. He called me Cel-es-tee every day and I felt like I was wasting his time. I wish I could've spoken up about it then. Maybe I would've passed my test."

"Forget him," she says. "You've been swimming with Grandad, right? And I've been driving with Grandad, so maybe now we can pass our tests."

I smile. I can't see her face, but I know she's smiling, too.

"I pranked you because I thought you were pranking me and I wanted to be like you," I say.

"I thought you said you thought I was mean. You wanted to be mean?"

"No . . . I don't know," I say.

Capri laughs again. "I'm loud but I'm not mean. At least not all the time. Or on purpose."

"I'm sorry for pranking you," I say.

"It's okay. I'm way over it now."

I can't help myself. "Are you sorry for pranking me?" I ask.

"Celeste, I told you I didn't do that."

"But . . . you saw the light, right?" I ask. "In the attic?"

"I did . . ." She trails off. She stops braiding for a second. "I kind of thought I imagined it until you said something about it again. I don't know what that's about, Celeste."

Now I feel uneasy again.

"Did you really prank Owen?" she asks. "Tell the truth. I won't tell anyone."

"I didn't," I say. "I don't know what that's about, either."

"Hm," she says. She braids again. "Hm."

We both sit in silence, thinking. Two unexplained situations.

Grandad and Owen come out as Capri finishes one half of my hairstyle. "Do you like this?" She hands me a small mirror and I look at the braid. I love it even more than the ones I had before.

"It's beautiful," I tell her.

She smiles. "Thanks. I know."

CHAPTER
9

I'd never thought I'd enjoy something like that, but it was almost like watching a movie. The sky changed from gray to navy blue to hues of pink and orange as the storm calmed down and the sun poked out a little before it set. After Capri finished my hair, I ran inside to grab my sketch pad and pencils. I did my best to draw the fast-moving clouds and rain. We counted the number of seconds between a lightning strike and a thunder boom, and even one thunder boom to the next, before both the thunder and lightning went away.

I stayed outside to finish my drawing, even when everyone else went inside. I walk in the house and look around the living room. It's cozy and a little small, and a little old-fashioned. No wonder Daisy sat in here so long during the thunderstorm, it seems like her style. There are a few photos around. There's one of Mama and Daddy at their wedding. It looks almost identical to the wedding photo of Grandma and Grandad in their room. There are other photos of Uncle Howard on what looks like a vacation. Uncle Steve and Aunt Marlene. My other aunt, Aunt Joanna, is holding her round belly. A new cousin will be born into our family soon.

Cousins. I remember what Grandma said about cousins being some of our first best friends. I think about Daisy, how afraid she was during the thunderstorm, and decide to check on her.

I pass Grandma, Grandad, and Owen at the kitchen table, nature books of all types spread out in front of them. We all smile at one another and I walk upstairs to Daisy's room and knock on her door. "Come in," she says. I open her door. She's sitting on her bed, writing. She looks upset still.

"Hey," I say, sitting down beside her. "Are you okay?"

She looks at me strangely and nods. She doesn't look okay. In her lap is a notebook covered in photos of lots of glamorous-looking women.

"That is Dorothy Dandridge, who Grandad was talking about," she says after she sees me staring. "And that's Lena Horne. And that's Diahann Carroll. Grandma told me that I have a big imagination, and when I'm afraid of something happening, I could write it down and turn it into a story instead." She shrugs. "I'm still afraid, but it's helping me a little."

"You look like these women," I tell her. In her newest polka-dot romper, Daisy looks like her photo would fit right along all of theirs. "And that's a really cool idea. Hey, maybe one day with my drawings and your stories, we could write a book together."

She smiles and nods.

"I can see how thunderstorms are scary," I keep going. "Nature can be unpredictable, huh?"

"But it's also beautiful," she says wistfully. "That's the catch."

"Well, I don't think you have anything to be afraid of," I continue on. "I guess if you're safe and take precautions, that's all you can do. Maybe one day you can enjoy them, even. What do you think?"

Daisy turns to look at me slowly.

"Okay, maybe that was a stretch," I say. "But—"

"You already said that," Daisy says.

"Said what?"

"That I can enjoy them."

"When did I say that?"

"Just a few moments ago," she says. "Remember?"

I think back to our short conversation and shake my head. "No, I just came inside. I sat out and sketched after Grandad, Capri, and Owen came back in."

"Before, when you came in to get your sketch pad?" Daisy asks. "When I was in the living room. Then you came and sat down and we talked for a little about thunderstorms and how I don't need to be afraid of the dark and the power going out. I said the power going out is one of my biggest fears because you can't see what's happening and someone could get hurt. Don't you remember?"

"I did come in to get my sketch pad, but we didn't talk at all," I say. "Wasn't Grandma sitting in there with you?"

"She was for a little while. Then you came."

I try to think. What was Daisy doing when I

came back downstairs with the sketch pad? I can't remember.

"That's strange," I say. First, Owen thought I pranked him and then Daisy thought I was talking to her. What's going on? Were they just dreaming?

And then the attic light. Capri admitted she saw it, too.

The attic . . . the box with the eyes peeking through the top.

Grandma being secretive.

The hairs on my arms stand up again. Something weird is going on in this house.

She furrows her eyebrows together. "You really don't remember?"

"Daisy," I say, scooting closer to her. "I need you to listen to me now. I wasn't talking to you downstairs and I didn't prank Owen. I've been hearing things, like someone whispering my name, and seeing lights where there shouldn't be."

"What do you think is going on?" she asks.

I can barely believe what I'm about to ask her.

"Daisy. Do you think this house could be haunted?"

Daisy lifts her eyebrows a little. "Haunted? You think Grandma and Grandad are living in a haunted house?"

"I don't know what's going on," I tell her.

She shrugs and stares at me with her big round eyes. "Anything is possible."

BOOM!

We hear a noise so loud the house shakes. Daisy and I look at each other. Is it storming again?

We hear it again. Daisy screams.

The windows blow open and a fierce wind comes in Daisy's room. The curtains whip through the air like arms, reaching toward us. A hard rain blows in, soaking the floor.

Another boom.

Daisy starts to cry.

I grab her hand. "Let's get out of here—now!"

I reach for the door and it flies open before I touch it, slamming against the wall. I see Capri, going down the steps when another BOOM makes her stumble forward.

I see the moment she loses her footing.

She reaches behind her, but no one is there.

Our eyes meet, hers full of confusion before she tumbles down the stairs.

"Capri!" I yell.

"Noo!" Daisy wails. She breaks her hand free from mine and runs down the stairs.

Capri lies at the bottom of the staircase holding her leg. Her leg! Her Olympic track star legs!

I run behind Daisy, skipping steps to get to the bottom faster. My heart pounds as I pray for her to be okay.

Grandma's eyes watch me until I reach the bottom step. She frowns.

"Celeste, how could you push your cousin down the stairs?"

CHAPTER 10

For a second, I'm so shocked I can't speak. Then I find my voice.

"Grandma, I would never do that!" I say.

"I saw you behind Capri on the steps right before she fell!" Grandma says.

"No, Grandma! I was just coming out of Daisy's room!"

I look at Daisy, frantic, and she nods. "It's true, Grandma! We were sitting on my bed when my windows blew open! Capri fell as soon as we came out of my room!"

We all look at Capri. Grandad is holding her leg, and when he lets go, she straightens it out and moves it around. I'm filled with relief. She has a nasty bruise, but it doesn't seem broken.

Capri gets up and hops from one foot to the other. She looks more relieved than I feel.

"It's funny that you said that, Grandma," Capri says. She looks at me.

Oh no. I hope she doesn't think I pushed her down, right when we were starting to become friends!

"Celeste, I thought I saw you behind me on the stairs, too." She shook her head. "But then I saw you come out of Daisy's room before I . . . fell." She looks up the stairs and then shakes her head again and rubs her knee.

Grandma's eyes widen as she looks at all of us and then, I realize, to the attic. She shakes her head.

"Of course. I must've been seeing things. I'm so sorry for accusing you, Celeste." She reaches in for a hug and squeezes me tight. "I should've never done that. I just thought—" She shakes her head again.

"It's okay, Grandma," I say. "It was a lot going on."

"Was it another storm?" Grandad says. "It seems like it's gone already."

We all listen. Sure enough, there are no more booms or sounds of heavy rain.

"It didn't sound like thunder to me," Owen says. "It sounded like a mountain lion roaring."

"I think it was raining, Owen," I say. "The windows and door in Daisy's room flew right open." I point up the stairs, right to Daisy's room, but I can see that her door is closed.

I climb a few steps to get a better view. "Daisy, did you close the door behind you?" I ask, feeling like I already know the answer.

She shakes her head, her eyes growing wider and wider.

I climb the rest of the steps and open Daisy's door. Her windows are closed. The curtains are neatly in place. The floor is dry.

I come back downstairs, shaking my head. "It's like nothing happened. Your floor is completely dry now."

"*Really?*" Daisy says. "After all that rain?"

Owen looks back and forth at us, then looks away, deep in thought. I know he's trying to think of an explanation for this, but there is none.

"Are you okay?" he asks Capri.

She nods, her bruise becoming more purple on her brown skin. "I'm fine."

"I think we've all had too much excitement for one day," Grandad says.

"I'm going to make a big pot of stew, some comfort food," Grandma says. "I'll holler for you when it's ready. Capri, come with me and let's get some ice on that knee."

"Daisy, come on upstairs and let's make sure those windows are locked tight," Grandad says.

Capri, Daisy, Owen, and I all look at one another. None of us know what to say, but by the look on all our faces, I think we can agree that something's not right.

Owen is staring at me with a confused, half-sleepy face. "You think this house is haunted?" he says again, stifling a yawn.

I nod. It's after dinner. None of us kids ate or talked as much as we normally do. I couldn't wait to get upstairs and tell Owen my theory about the house being haunted.

"I don't know, Celeste."

"Come on, Owen," I say. "What are the odds of you

and Daisy saying she saw me somewhere that I wasn't? Grandma was sure she saw me push Capri! Even Capri had second thoughts!" He blinks at me. He probably can't believe that I haven't admitted to pranking him yet. Even though I know I didn't.

"Daisy *does* have a big imagination. And Capri might've been confused with all the commotion—"

I groan. "Why can't you believe me? I thought you said you watched a show where some guys searched a haunted hotel?"

"Yes, but they had evidence. They had this special device that recorded these sound waves to determine that there were ghosts everywhere."

"Where in the world would I get that?"

Owen shrugs. "I don't know. Maybe we could find some other proof."

I sigh. Owen just looks at me.

"I don't believe you're making it up, Celeste," he says. "It's just hard to believe. And scary, too. I mean, what would we do if this house really was haunted?"

I get it. No one wants to believe that they are living with ghosts. But now it's all I can think about.

"Let's get some sleep and talk about it more in the morning," Owen says. "Promise."

Owen turns over and falls asleep at the end of my bed. I crawl in at the head of it, listening for any signs of ghosts.

Something makes me jump straight up out of bed and I can't remember what it was. Was it a sound? I look at Owen and he's snoring lightly.

Something glimmers out of the corner of my eye.

A light, shining from under my bedroom door. Is someone in the hallway?

I open the door and see the light is coming from above me. The attic.

I stare at it for a second to make sure that it's real. Sure enough, the light is seeping from the corners of the attic door. I hear Owen snore again. Should I wake him up and show him? So he can believe me?

If I can convince a grown-up, then everyone will believe me. I look at the staircase, to the pitch-black at the bottom.

I take a deep breath and walk down the staircase as fast and carefully as I can. I think of how Capri slipped and hurt her leg earlier. How Grandma thought I pushed her. How Celeste thought someone was standing right behind her.

Whatever is going on around here, it's getting dangerous.

The thought makes me look over my shoulder as I walk down the staircase. My stomach flips. I don't know what I might find.

But all I see is that light coming from the attic, brighter than ever.

Once I'm downstairs, I see the moonlight casting big strips of light through the dark living room and kitchen. I walk faster toward Grandma and Grandad's room, my feet making tap tap sounds on the floor.

I push their door open. It's quiet. I walk over to their bed, stepping carefully in the dark.

"Grandad?" I say as I get closer.

But it's Grandma whose eyes snap open and who turns toward me.

"I didn't mean to wake you—" I start.

Grandma furrows her brow and shakes her head. "Ellie, what are you doing in here?"

Ellie? Grandma must be dreaming about her sister. Even though her eyes are open and she's looking at me. Is she talking in her sleep? I heard you weren't supposed to wake up sleepwalkers. I need to wake Grandad.

"Ellie, I know you hear me talking to you," she says again.

"I'm not—"

"You need to stop scaring these kids."

My heart thumps in my chest. "What—what kids?"

"My grandchildren are starting to notice you and you hurt my eldest one today. I scolded Celeste for no reason. This has to stop, now. We've been through this before. You need to rest."

I feel dizzy and sweaty. Grandma thinks I'm Ellie.

That's why Owen and Daisy and even Grandma thought they saw me when they didn't.

They saw someone who looks just like me.

A ghost.

Great-Aunt Ellie.

"I—I—" I don't know what to say or what to do. Great-Aunt Ellie's ghost is here? And Grandma knows it?

Tears fall out of my eyes. Is that why Grandma doesn't want to talk about Great-Aunt Ellie? Because she's haunting this house?

"J-Judy?" I say. It feels weird calling Grandma by her first name, to pretend to be someone that I'm not. It reminds me of when I tried to become a prankster. "What happened to me?"

"You've always tried so hard to be fearless and you've always just been *reckless*. Listen to me, Celestine. You've done enough."

"No, I mean how—how did I—?"

"Celeste?"

A deeper voice cuts through the darkness. Grandad.

A lamp cuts on, showing Grandad's sleepy face and Grandma's surprised one.

"Celeste, what's wrong?" he asks.

Grandma blinks at me with an embarrassed look on her face and rubs her hand across her eyes. "Oh my, was I talking in my sleep again?"

I don't know if Grandma really thinks she was talking in her sleep or if she thinks she was talking to Ellie. I decide to play along.

"Yes, Grandma."

If she was awake, she'd know that I was pretending to be Ellie to get answers. I try to read her face, but I can't tell what she's thinking.

"Celeste, what are you doing down here?" Grandma asks. "Are you crying?"

I realize my face is wet and I'm shaking a little bit.

"Um. I came down here to tell you that—" I stop. Now I know that Ellie is haunting this house, and that Grandma knows it, too. What should I say? If Grandma won't admit it or do anything about it, how could anything I say make a difference? And somehow I know that the light will be off when I go back upstairs.

"—that I had a bad dream."

"Oh, Celeste," Grandma says, shaking her head. She's probably thinking of the conversation she thought she had with Ellie.

"I'm sorry to hear that," Grandad says. "Would you like to sleep in the bed with us?"

I consider it, but what if Grandma starts talking to me like I'm Ellie again? The thought makes me shiver.

"I'm okay now," I say. "Thanks, Grandad. Good night, Grandma."

"Well, if you're sure," Grandad says. Grandma still looks shaken up, but she says good night and Grandad turns off his light.

I walk out, catching a glimpse of the photo of Great-Aunt Ellie on the dresser. I study it for a second, to see if it moves. It doesn't.

I walk back to the staircase and sure enough, the light is off.

CHAPTER 11

I run back upstairs and wake up Capri, Daisy, and Owen, and we gather in my room. Once everyone's sitting on my bed, I tell them everything that happened downstairs with Grandma and Grandad. About Great-Aunt Ellie.

"It all makes sense," I continue. "Daisy, you thought I was talking to you yesterday when I was actually outside. Grandma thought I pushed Capri. Owen thought I pranked him. All this time, it wasn't me, but the ghost of Great-Aunt Ellie."

Everyone is looking at me talk, but nobody is interrupting me. I take this as a good sign that they believe me.

I pace the floor. "Daisy and I saw the windows blow open. We *heard* them open. We felt the rain! But after Capri fell, it was like it never happened!"

Capri's mouth is open in shock. Owen closes his eyes and scrunches his face up like he's trying to think.

"And think about the attic light. I saw it with my own eyes, but I also saw Grandad try to fix it. There's no source of light in there. You saw the light, too, right, Capri?"

She nods. "I did."

I think some more. "There was a box up there, a box that Grandad didn't want me to see. He said there's some information about Great-Aunt Ellie in there. We need to find out more about who she is and why she's haunting us."

I take a deep breath.

"We need to go to the attic."

It wasn't scary when I went with Grandad. But now that I know there's a ghost in this house . . . one that doesn't hesitate to push Capri down the stairs or throw heavy boots at Owen . . . it could be a different story. Especially because we don't know what's in that box.

"I don't get it. Why would Grandma and Grandad stay in a haunted house?" Capri asks.

"Maybe she isn't haunting them," Daisy says. "Or

maybe just because the house is haunted now, that doesn't mean it's always been haunted. Maybe she is haunting *us*."

"I've never had a ghost haunt me," Owen pipes up. "Right, Celeste?"

"Well, don't look at me," Capri says. She holds up her hands, smirking. "Celeste, you're the one with the dead lady look-alike. Maybe you're not even Celeste." She pokes a finger toward me. "Maybe you're the ghost."

"Stop it," I say, hugging myself. I know I'm not a ghost.

Capri reaches out and squeezes my arm. She tries to smile like she was joking, but I wonder if she really needed to make sure that I'm the real Celeste.

"She's not just a dead lady, that's our great-aunt," Owen says. "And plus, she was only a little girl when she died."

"Grandma said, 'You've always been fearless, but now you're getting reckless.' I think Grandma knows she might hurt us." I still pace the floor, back and forth, back and forth. "Think about what happened with Capri. Luckily, she only got a bruise, but it could've been worse. And maybe it *could* get worse. If we don't stop her."

"How do we stop her?" Daisy asks.

"I don't know," I admit. "But I do know that Grandad and Grandma have been secretive about her and how she died. And Grandad was secretive about what was in that box. If we go to the attic, maybe it'll give us some clues."

We all sit in silence for a second, thinking. Light leaks in through my bedroom window. We've been talking for so long, the sun has already started to rise.

Rap rap rap.

There's a sharp, quick knock at the door. We look at one another. Who could it be, this early in the morning?

"Come in," I say.

It's Grandad. "I'm sorry to disturb you all, but I wanted to ask Capri if she was up for an early morning drive?"

Capri's eyes stretch wide and she shakes her head. "No, sir. Maybe later," she says.

Grandad just smiles and nods and closes the door.

"Grandad wants to take me driving while it's early and no one else is on the road," Capri says, explaining herself. "I'm, um, still a little sleepy. I can't drive while I'm sleepy."

I look at Capri, but she averts her eyes. I wonder if she's still a little afraid that she's going to mess up. Or afraid of all this talk of ghosts.

There's another knock at the door, but this one is so hard, it makes the door shake.

BOOM. BOOM. BOOM!

Owen goes to open it. It's probably Grandad again.

But no one is there.

"Hello?" he says, looking up and down the hallway. "No one." He tries to shrug it off, but I know my brother. He doesn't like not having an explanation.

We see a flicker of light above Owen's head.

The attic.

I jump up, my heart beating fast.

"Okay, so now you see it for yourself!" I say.

This house is haunted!

"It—it has to be a faulty light or—or a reflection," Owen says. "Maybe the sunlight?"

Owen looks at me, but I shake my head.

"Celeste," he whispers. "What's going on? What do we do?"

"She already told us," Daisy says. Her voice makes me jump. She's not sitting on the bed anymore, but standing by my dresser. She reminds me of our kitten back at home. You don't hear her come into a room or leave, but she's always there, watching everything.

"Celeste is right. We have to go to the attic."

We hear an engine start in the distance. Grandad must be going somewhere. It's so early, we don't even hear Grandma starting breakfast yet.

I look at Owen. He looks as nervous as I feel.

I force myself to stand up straighter. "If we're going to do it, we should do it now, before Grandma starts moving around."

The attic light flickers off and on again as we walk into the hallway.

CHAPTER 12

"Is anyone afraid?" I ask.

Owen and Capri shake their heads, but I can't tell if they're telling the truth or not.

"Grandma said she wasn't scary, remember?" Daisy says.

"So, let me get this straight," Capri says. "You're afraid of thunderstorms but not the possibility of talking to a ghost?"

"Well, it's not really the storms I'm afraid of, it's the possibility of the power going out or someone getting hurt," Daisy says.

"And that kind of already happened," Capri tells her, pointing toward her knee. "The getting hurt part."

Daisy shrugs. "Yeah. It's just like how you're not

really afraid of driving, you're just afraid of messing up, because you like to be perfect."

"Who told you that?" Capri says, narrowing her eyes.

"Um. I thought it was Celeste, but now I'm not so sure."

"Well, now that we have that out of the way," Capri says, rolling her eyes. "It feels like we're stalling. Let's do this."

Capri runs to her room and comes back out with her cell phone and a chair. She turns on the flashlight app.

"Spot me, Celeste," Capri says. I hold the chair still while Capri stands on top, grabs the string, and pulls the attic door down. It creaks open and the steps lead to what looks like a black hole in the ceiling.

She shines her phone into the attic. It gives us a small view, but it's still pretty dark.

"Creepy," Owen says.

Capri takes a deep breath and hoists herself up. She grunts a little bit, and muscles pop out of her arms and legs. "You come, Celeste, then we can help Daisy up and Owen can come up last."

We help one another up and look around the cramped, hot space.

"And Grandad said there was no light switch?" Owen asks.

"Nope. No bulb, either," I say.

Owen doesn't say anything.

We each walk around the attic. I try to remember exactly which box it was that I'm thinking of. I know it was by the window. It's hard to see anything the farther we get from the attic door with the weak light that filters in from downstairs. It's cloudy, so even the small window isn't giving us much light.

There are boxes everywhere. Owen stumbles into one, and the sound makes us all jump.

My foot hits a really worn-looking box. I open it and it's a jumble of random items: shoes and old clothes that look like they belong to a little girl. Maybe these were my mom's things.

The attic gets a shade darker.

"Let's move on," I say.

Owen grabs another box and opens it, throwing things around. It just looks like a bunch of Christmas decorations.

"Nothing," he says.

Finally, I see what looks like the box I saw when I was up here with Grandad.

"There it is," I say. I wonder what we'll find.

We open the box. I don't see the pair of eyes staring at me like I did before. There are a bunch of old newspapers and photo albums.

We pull out a big tan photo album and a few newspapers. The photo album is worn; some of the edges are coming off and it seems like the cover is hanging on by a thread. I open it.

I see a picture of what looks like Grandma Judy, holding hands with a little girl who looks a little older than her. Capri flashes her phone over the picture.

"Wow," I whisper.

"Celeste," Daisy says. "She really looks so much like you."

"Maybe there's more," Capri says. "Turn the page."

I turn the page and shriek, dropping the book.

There is a huge black-and-white photo of me covering the entire right side of the album—I mean, of Great-Aunt Ellie. We can see every detail of her face. Her braids—they are the exact same style that Capri braided my hair in yesterday. The other photos I've seen match the hairstyle I had before. Everything, even the mole above her eyebrow, even her *teeth*, are exactly like mine. It's like her photos are changing to look more like me.

"Whoa," Owen, Daisy, and Capri all say in unison.

I look at the photo from another angle. My eyes—*her* eyes—seem to follow me.

"This is uncanny," Daisy says.

"Celeste . . . This isn't you . . . right?" Owen asks.

"Of course it's not me," I say, but even I have my doubts. I have to remind myself that I've never taken this picture.

I shiver. "Let's look at something else," I say, slamming the book closed.

Suddenly, a piece of sun peeks through the clouds and gives us a streak of light that lands right on an old-looking green chest. I don't remember seeing it the first time I was in here with Grandad.

"Look at that old chest near the window," Capri says. "Maybe she's sitting on it and we just don't see her." She laughs, but I get the feeling she's a little nervous.

We walk over to the chest. Capri and I try to pull open the rusted latch, but it doesn't budge. It's locked.

I sigh, disappointed.

A bright light washes over me, so bright I have to shield my eyes, and flickers off again. Capri and I look at each other. Her eyes are wide.

"Did you see that?" we both say to each other.

"Where did that come from?" Owen says, looking at the ceiling.

The light flickers bright and quick, like a camera flash. It comes through the cracks in the floor, the walls. It comes from nowhere and everywhere.

Daisy screams.

"Let's get out of here," Capri says, standing up and grabbing my hand. We run forward, reaching out for Owen and Daisy.

SLAM!

The chest flips open and papers fly everywhere.

"What's happening?" Daisy screams again.

The lights continue to flicker. The papers drop to the ground with a thud, like they're heavy. The light goes out again.

Shaking, I drop Capri's hand and reach for one of the papers.

"Celeste, don't touch it!" Owen yells. "Paper shouldn't land hard like that!"

"I have to!" I say, my voice quivering. "We have to find out what's going on here!"

My eyes focus on the papers—they are photos. There's a black-and-white photo of what instantly looks like a young Grandad. One where he's posing by a pool sign that says COLOREDS ONLY. One where he's riding a horse. Another where he is playing in a field with his hat on.

I find another one. This one looks like a younger picture of Grandma, standing on the steps of a small house, dressed up in a sash and a crown, as if she were in a beauty pageant.

"Hey, look at this!" Capri says. She waves a flashlight over a newspaper clipping spread out in front of her.

I walk over to the clipping and see the headline.

COLORED GIRL DROWNS IN LAKESIDE COMMUNITY.

"Colored girl?" Capri asks, sucking her teeth. "Really?"

Owen steps forward and leans over the article. "This article is about Great-Aunt Ellie."

We all lean over one another, scanning the article.

"It says that she drowned in a lake only a few days after she was removed from a local community pool for being Black," Daisy says. "Wow."

My heart thumps. It reminds me of the woman who wanted Grandad and me to leave the community pool a few days ago.

"It looks like she was trying to take swimming lessons, but they were only offering them on the days of the week when the pool was for Whites only," Owen says. "Fridays."

We sit in silence, scanning the article. I may have failed my swimming lesson, but Great-Aunt Ellie didn't even get a chance to have one because of the color of her skin.

"That's not fair!" Capri yells. I'm shocked to see that there are tears falling down Capri's cheeks. Mine too. "She didn't deserve to die."

We flip the pages of the article and I expect to see my own mirror image staring up at me, but nothing. "There's no picture of her," I mutter.

"No! It's like they didn't even care," Capri says again, sobbing. I wipe the tears from my own eyes and pick up another article. This time, it's Grandad. There's a picture of him. He is a younger man in this article, and he is holding up the photo of himself on lifeguard duty when he was in his teens. I notice this is a different newspaper, too. In this one, there seems to be only Black people through the pages. All their names are printed in the articles, and every article has photos.

JIMMY HAWTHORNE IS DEDICATED TO POOL SAFETY.

All four of us lean in to read the article. In this one, Grandad talks about how he has always loved the water and has dedicated his life to teaching young Black kids how to swim. He talks about meeting Grandma after hearing about what happened to her sister, them getting married, and then—

When I read it, I gasp.

"'Jimmy and Judy decided to build a house on the same lake Judy's sister, Celestine, drowned in.'"

"People thought it was strange to do that," Grandad is quoted saying, "but we felt it was a way to honor

Celestine. Plus, Judy felt that it brought her closer to her sister."

We all turn to look at one another.

No wonder Great-Aunt Ellie is haunting this place.

She died here.

CHAPTER 13

"Kids!" we hear a voice calling us.

Grandad.

"Kids, what are you doing up there?"

"Let's get out of here," Capri says.

As afraid as I am, I don't want to leave yet. I need to find out more information. I need to think. What if as easily as this information came to us, it goes away again? I need to know more.

And I think it's time that I ask Grandma.

One by one, we climb down the ladder and Capri closes the attic door. Then we run downstairs.

Grandad is standing at the bottom of the stairs. "Were you kids in the attic?" he asks. "I thought I saw a light flashing in there."

"Yes, Grandad," I say, trying to catch my breath. "Where's Grandma?"

"She's in the kitchen," Grandad says. "What's wrong? Why, you look like you just saw a ghost."

"I think we did, Grandad," Daisy says.

"What in the world?" I hear Grandad's confused voice and heavy footsteps follow us to the kitchen as we run to Grandma. She turns around, smiling, but then furrows her eyebrows when she sees us breathing hard.

"What's going on?"

"Grandma?" I ask. I stand up, clear my throat, and look her straight in the eye.

"Grandma, did Great-Aunt Ellie drown in that lake?" I point to it, right outside our window.

Grandma looks at me, then Grandad.

"You built a house where your sister died?" Capri asks, shaking her head. "Why, Grandma?"

Grandma sighs, a deep long sigh, like she's been carrying a weight that she just let go.

"Well, like I told you, when we were kids, we weren't really allowed to swim. Everywhere you went, there were pools with signs on them that said Whites Only.

When the pools were finally supposed to desegregate, a lot of them just closed down instead because people still didn't want to swim with Black kids. It made us sad. Ellie and I always talked about being world travelers. We talked about jumping off cliffs into bodies of clear water, swimming in the Pacific Ocean . . . But we still didn't know how to. One day, we found an open pool that Black kids could swim in! We stayed close to the edge and waded and had a ball. Then some older White kids came and taunted us so bad . . . splashing us and saying how dirty the pool was because we were in it. Ooh, your great-aunt Ellie was furious. She was determined to learn how to swim after that, but she never wanted to go to that pool again because we were disrespected. What were we supposed to do? Our parents didn't know how to swim, their parents didn't know how, none of our friends did. Who would teach us? Where could we learn?

"One day, Ellie had the idea to . . . teach herself. There was a lake that anyone could go to. It was an awful idea. I tried my best to talk her out of it, I really did. But once Ellie had an idea, well, you couldn't talk her out of it. She went in the lake and . . . I wanted to go out and save her but I couldn't . . . I didn't . . ."

Now Grandma has tears in her eyes. Grandad hugs her, while Owen reaches out and touches her arm.

"It's what Ellie wanted," Grandma says. "Truly, it's what she wanted. She always said she wanted to be buried by the lake. I just wish it wasn't as soon as it was, and I wish it didn't happen the way it did. But I know my sister. That's what she wanted."

I feel so sorry for Grandma, and even Great-Aunt Ellie. All she wanted to do was swim.

"Why didn't you tell us this before?" I ask her.

"Because I felt like you would be afraid," she says. "Celeste, I knew that you were having trouble learning how to swim, and I didn't want the news that your great-aunt drowned to discourage you from learning. In fact, I hoped that you would be proud to learn, to do something your great-aunt wanted to do so badly and couldn't."

In the attic, when I first learned that Great-Aunt Ellie couldn't take swimming lessons, it made me feel like I had to learn how to swim to honor her. But now that

I know she drowned here, in this lake, it does make me feel that I should stay away from it, too. I don't tell Grandma this.

"But aren't you afraid?" Daisy asks. "What if her ghost haunted—"

"Your great-aunt is *not* a ghost," Grandma says, her voice getting firm. "She is my sister, a real person. And even if she was, she wouldn't haunt me. She loved me and she would love all of you."

"But, Grandma," I say. "I saw—"

Daisy touches my hand and shakes her head. I want to keep going, to tell her that I realized that she was talking to Great-Aunt Ellie thinking it was me, telling her to stop doing mean things to us. She is haunting us and Grandma knows she is.

I think about what Grandad said. *It'll always be enough for the right people at the right time.* Maybe now isn't the right time.

The kitchen is quiet. Everyone looks at one another.

Grandad clears his throat. "Well now, how about some fresh air after being in that stuffy attic? Celeste, you want to head out to the pool after breakfast?"

I don't. Now that I know why Great-Aunt Ellie is here, I want to know more. Did these kinds of things always happen, and our grandparents just ignored it, or didn't notice? Or is it only happening now because we're here? And if so, what does she want from us?

I remember Grandma telling her, *You need to rest.* How can we get her to do that before she pushes Capri again? Or worse?

But I'm not going to get any more answers from Grandma right now, and she probably won't want us to go back into the attic today.

I catch Capri's eye and she nods at me. As much as I want to stay away from the pool, I need to get out of this house.

Maybe being at the pool will give me some time to think.

———

Grandad and I are at the pool. I'm doing so much better, dog-paddling to Grandad and even jumping in his arms in the pool. Now Grandad is asking me to jump in the pool by myself.

"You just seem like you're getting so comfortable wading around," he says. "I think you can do it."

It's a bright and sunny day, only white, fluffy clouds in the sky. No gray ones. No sign of a storm forcing us out of the water.

I look around. There are a bunch of people in and around the pool, but no one seems to care that we are here.

This is big. I've never done this before, not even during swimming lessons back home.

"I'll be right here, not letting you out of my sight," Grandad says.

I nod at him and take a deep breath. "Okay," I say.

"On the count of three," Grandad says. "One, two . . ."

I pinch my nose with my fingers.

It feels like all the noise in the world stops as my head goes under. I don't even open my eyes.

As soon as I feel my feet touch the ground, I push back up to the surface, not even letting go of my nose until I'm sure I'm completely out of the water. I hate the feeling of water getting in my nose.

I open my eyes slowly, the water running down my face. I take a deep breath.

"That's my girl! You did it!" Grandad says, smiling. I like how he is letting me go at my own pace, unlike Stinky-Breath Jared, who would've been annoyed at how long I'm taking to get used to the water.

I smile back at him. Even though I am still getting used to the pool, it's a small accomplishment.

———

Everyone cheers for me at dinner when Grandad tells them what I did. I smile.

"Thanks, everyone," I say. I can't wait to tell Mama and Daddy. They'll be so proud of me.

"We started to hike the trail today, but Owen thought he heard something growling and we turned back around," Capri says.

I look at my brother. "Is that true?"

He shrugs. "Yeah. I figured it was best to turn around before we got in too deep and saw a mountain lion, right? Hey, can you pass the green beans?"

I pass them to him, but my eyebrows furrow a little.

It doesn't seem to bother him that he's afraid of hiking, but I think he's trying to make excuses.

He's silent for a second, like he's thinking. Then he shrugs. "I just don't see why it's important for me to hike."

"Well," I say, "you love the outdoors. It seems like something you would really love if it weren't for the mountain lion thing."

"Sure. But we have a backyard. And I go to the lake."

"There are plenty of trails that don't have mountain lions on them," I say. "You can just research those or take precautions whenever you do hike. Remember, you're not even afraid of hiking, just the idea of running into a mountain lion."

"Hmm, that's true. What other places should I avoid to decrease my chances of running into a mountain lion?"

"Owen. That's not what I meant."

"You'll thank me," he says, between bites of his green beans, "if we narrowly escape the jaws of a mountain lion because of my safety precautions."

I laugh and talk with my family, but my mind keeps drawing to what we saw earlier. I look out at the sun setting on the lake, and think about Great-Aunt Ellie. The table gets quiet, and I look at Daisy, Capri, and Owen. I know they're thinking about it, too. We're living with a ghost. How do we get her to go away?

Upstairs, we all leave our doors open. I hear the record player in Daisy's room, and start to hum and dance a little bit along to it. I wonder if this was the kind of music Great-Aunt Ellie listened to. Did she hum and dance to the music the same way I am right now? She probably looked just like me doing it. The thought makes me stop.

I try to draw to get my mind off everything. I grab my sketchbook and continue drawing my picture of the lake. I add a drawing of Great-Aunt Ellie, about to jump in. I draw her looking back to the house, maybe at Grandma, her smile to the side, a crooked one that makes her look sneaky.

I picture myself making that same face. It doesn't even feel natural.

What do you want, Great-Aunt Ellie? I think. *Why are you bothering us?*

CHAPTER 14

I tossed and turned for hours last night. I stayed up, listening for footsteps creaking, my name being whispered, or the attic light turning on while everyone else was asleep.

When I did fall asleep, I had the same bad dream again. I was falling, falling, and the body of water I was in was bigger than ever before. When I jumped up, it was already morning and very hot.

Grandma asked everyone to come to the lake with her at breakfast. I think she wants to make sure we aren't afraid of it because of what we found out yesterday. I definitely didn't want to go, but I went with them because I didn't want to be the only one in the house in case Great-Aunt Ellie showed up.

So now I'm outside, the combination of the cool lake

air and the hot sun feeling good on my skin. The sun shines so bright against the lake, I have to squint and shield my eyes. I see the dock and Grandad's precious boats beside it.

Owen walks up beside me, his life jacket already on. He hands one to me. I look at the water. It reminds me of my dream. Of Great-Aunt Ellie.

I shake my head.

"I'm not getting in the water," I tell him. I don't even know why I bothered to put on my swimsuit. Or grab a towel.

"That's okay," he says. He puts the life jacket down and runs onto the dock with Grandma and Daisy. I notice that the dock rocks from side to side. He jumps in.

"Be careful, Owen!" I say. My heart beats faster. Well, at least he has on his life jacket. He can swim, and Grandma and Daisy can swim, too. So he should be okay. If I fell in, it could be different.

The thought makes me put on the life jacket Owen left.

"Wow! Come on, Celeste!" Owen says, swimming back up to the dock. "You have to see this school of fish swimming by the dock!"

"No," I say, backing away from the lake.

"You don't have to get in!" he yells back.

Grandma and Daisy yell for me to come toward them on the dock. I grab my arms.

I keep thinking about how I fell in my dream. It was a big body of water, just like this.

You can do it, I say to myself. *You're not getting in. You have on your life jacket. It's okay.*

I walk on the dock. It instantly rocks a little to the side. I grab the railing.

It's okay, I think.

I take one step after another and soon I'm at the edge of the dock with everyone.

"I'm glad you're here, baby," Grandma says. "Quick, look at those fish."

Sure enough, there's a large school of fish, swimming together underwater. There has to be at least a hundred of them. I watch them swimming as one. It reminds me of what my grandma says about how all of us cousins should stick together.

"Isn't it cool?" Owen says. "Fish swim in schools because it helps protect them from predators."

"Yes, there can be safety in numbers," Grandma says.

I watch the fish, and slowly I start to see my own reflection in the lake. The more I look at it, the more the facial expression doesn't look like mine, but like the sneaky smile that Great-Aunt Ellie has.

This starts to annoy me. I can't get away from her face, especially since it's my own. I don't want to think about what happened to her in this lake. I turn away and walk toward the house.

Suddenly, the dock shakes violently. I yell out and grab at the railing. Even still, I slip and fall. When I try to get up again, it shakes worse and I thud back down to my knees. I'm going to slide right into the lake! I try again and again to stand up, but I can't. I slide along the slippery wood surface, and my leg swings out and over the water—my toes, then my foot, dipping below the surface. My fingers are digging into the wood but I'm starting to lose my grip—

It stops.

I yank my leg back onto the dock and huddle there for a moment, breathless. I'm soaked in sweat and lake water. I'm still afraid to stand up, but I cautiously push onto all fours. I look around to see if everyone is okay, and they're all swimming out past the dock, still looking at the fish. They're shouting and laughing. They didn't feel that?

"Did you all see that?" I yell. I stand up finally, feeling dizzy, a little afraid, and even a little angry. Why didn't they try to help me?

This gets everyone's attention. "See what?" Owen says.

See what? I shake my head. "Nothing." I don't feel like explaining it. I walk back toward the house.

The closer I get, I can see the balcony outside my bedroom, and the sketch pad I left there. I look above my room—the attic. I see my reflection in the attic window, my face as wide-eyed and shaken as I feel.

Wait a minute. The window isn't angled down at all—how can I see my reflection in the attic window?

My face breaks into a big smile, winks, and disappears from the window.

I scream, backing up on the dock, which is wobbly under my feet. I fall backward.

"Celeste! Are you okay?" Grandma asks.

"I—my face—somebody's up there!" I yell. "In the attic!"

"Oh, Celeste, that's probably just a trick of the light," Grandma says.

"No," I say, my body shaking. Grandma knows Great-Aunt Ellie's here! Why won't she just admit it? "No, Grandma!"

Owen looks at me and then looks at the attic. He squints and tilts his head for a long time, like he's trying to see something. "I don't see anything, Celeste," he says. I notice he doesn't say he doesn't believe me, which I appreciate. His eyes grow wide. "Hey, do you think it was—"

"There's nothing there," Grandma says. But she doesn't look up. "Maybe we are all getting hungry for lunch and it's time to go inside."

"But we just ate breakfast not too long ago," Capri says.

"The lake air does that to you," Grandma says, already striding out of the water and grabbing her towel. "Makes you hungry. Come on, let's go."

"Grandma," I say. She looks at me, holding my gaze. I try to read her eyes—does she remember talking to me the other night, thinking it was Great-Aunt Ellie? Does she know that *I* know the truth?

She looks at me, her eyes filled with sadness and something else I can't put my finger on. "Come on, baby," she says, and walks toward the house.

I keep my eye on the attic window, but I don't see anything. I know that Great-Aunt Ellie is up there. Grandma knows I'm telling the truth—and won't admit it. How long can she let this go on? I know she loves her sister, but we are all at risk of getting hurt!

"I'm sorry I didn't see anything, Celeste," Owen says. "But I believe you. What can we do?"

"Let's talk about it after lunch," I mutter. "I don't want Grandma to know what we're up to."

Grandma might not think her sister is dangerous, but I do. She pushed Capri down the stairs. She threw things at Owen. She tried to knock me into the water. To drown me. And it's time to stop her.

Daisy stops walking and turns around, waiting on me to catch up.

"Celeste," she says. "I saw her, too."

CHAPTER 15

"She's in the attic. We need to go there and figure out what she wants!" I say, more bravely than I feel. It's after lunch and we're all in my room again.

Capri scoffs. "Why would you want to go to her?"

"Well, I—" Capri has a point. She's done things that really could have hurt us. What if she goes further this time? "Because how do we know she won't stop haunting us? It's better to go to her than to lie awake in bed every night thinking she's going to hurt us again."

"Celeste, think!" Capri yells.

"I am thinking," I tell her.

"I'm sorry," she says, taking a deep breath. "It's just . . . I'm scared for you. You look just like her and she keeps showing up, pretending to be you. Maybe she wants to take your place."

We all stare at one another after this.

"Take—take my place?" I ask.

Capri shrugs. "Sure. Grandma and Grandad never said anything about the house being haunted. Our parents would have never sent us here if it were haunted when they were little, right? You saw how mad Grandma was when she thought it was you who pushed me down the stairs. Maybe Ellie wants to lock you up in the attic and take your place."

I'm speechless. Is that what she wants?

How can we stop her?

"At least we're leaving here in a couple of days," Owen says. "Then we won't have to think about this anymore."

I shake my head. "I don't want to take any chances and have her follow us home. What if she tries to take my place at home?" I shiver, just thinking about it. "We need to figure this out."

"We know Grandma knows she's here. Maybe she can just tell her to stop," says Daisy.

"Grandma thinks Great-Aunt Ellie can do no wrong," I tell her. "She knows about Ellie, I *know* she does, but she won't admit it. We need Grandma to see the truth, and to see that *we* know the truth. That way, she'll have no choice but to help us."

It's quiet as everyone thinks. "It seems like Great-Aunt Ellie only comes around when Celeste isn't there." Owen says. "Let's make it seem like Celeste is busy doing something and give Great-Aunt Ellie the chance to try and prank us. We call Grandma to help, then Celeste can come into the room."

"And once we're all there, Grandma can't deny what's going on in front of us," I say. "Good idea, Owen." He smiles at me.

We hear a knock at the door, and we all jump.

"Who is it?" I ask.

"It's Grandad! I wanted to see if you wanted to go to the pool again?"

I sigh in relief. "Um. Sure. Just a second! We're just . . . talking about something."

"No rush. I'll be downstairs whenever you're ready." I hear his footsteps going downstairs.

"Okay." I look around at my cousins and brother. "Let's brainstorm."

On the way to the pool, Grandad tells me how he and Grandma are going on a date tonight. They put Capri in charge to watch us while they're gone.

"Grandma and I go to the movies every Friday night," he says as he puts his key in the lock in the gate and we enter the pool area. "We've been doing it for fifty years."

"That's sweet," I say, grabbing on to the rail and stepping into the water. My mind is spinning. We're going to be alone tonight? What if Great-Aunt Ellie attacks us again without Grandma or Grandad there? I get a chill down my spine thinking about it. I hope our plan works when I get back to the house.

I see the pool water and it calms me down, just a little.

I'm realizing that being in the water actually helps me think, almost like drawing. It's not something I would've realized without Grandad's help. I tell him this. The way he smiles when I say this tells me that it made his day. I'm starting to like these pool days with Grandad.

"Y'all will have fun," I tell him. "We will probably watch some movies or something together at home."

I see someone behind Grandad walking into the pool. It's the woman who yelled at Grandad the other day and her daughter, Sarah.

I start to feel uncomfortable. What if she yells at us again?

I catch the eye of the little girl, and she waves at me. I offer a half smile back, but I don't feel like waving.

"What's the matter?" Grandad says, looking behind me. Then he sees them. "They won't bother us any-more," he says. "Are you ready?"

"Not really," I say, losing my nerve. I just need to forget about her and Great-Aunt Ellie for a second and focus on the pool.

Grandad and I work on some of the things Jared and I worked on, like my kicking. I get to the point where I can tread water and even do some front strokes to Grandad. It's the most comfortable I've ever felt in the pool.

"You're a natural," Grandad says when I reach him, and he looks so proud of me.

Maybe swimming is not so bad after all.

"I want to tread water again," I say. I'm actually starting to think it's fun.

"Be my guest," he says. I start treading water, feeling it swirl around my legs.

I look up and the older woman is glaring at me, all hate in her eyes.

It catches me off guard, and I stop treading and start sputtering.

I shiver. Grandma says we can pray to protect ourselves from evil ghosts. I wonder if the same thing applies to evil people. I try it.

Soon, my head is under the water.

Hold your breath, I think, but I still swallow some.

I'm yanked out of the water.

"Celeste! Are you okay?" Grandad says, patting my back. I cough a little.

I think about how Grandma said those boys chased her and Great-Aunt Ellie out of the pool. What if one of them was this lady's grandad and that's why she wants to do the same to me?

"Yeah. I think I'm just ready to stop," I say. I look up

and the woman is gone. I see the little girl closing the gate.

"Okay. Well, you did a great job today," he says, and he even sounds like he still believes it. I keep thinking about Great-Aunt Ellie. I wonder how she'd feel knowing I let that woman distract me in the pool. I guess I shouldn't swim when I'm distracted.

I can't believe the woman is still mad at us. Oh well. I guess it's like what I told Daisy about storms. I can take precautions, but I don't have to be afraid of her. I can keep swimming and having fun and doing anything else. I'll be back at the pool in no time, because I can be.

I think about the day I stood up to her. I still feel like I said the right things, and even at the right time. Maybe it was just the wrong person.

CHAPTER 16

We make our plan. When Grandma starts cooking dinner, I'll announce, loudly and clearly, that I'm getting in the shower. Then I'll turn the shower on so Grandma can know I'm in the bathroom. I'll be totally out of sight, since it seems like Great-Aunt Ellie always comes around pretending to be me when she knows I'm out of the way.

I'm just sitting in my room, waiting to hear Grandma. I get bored, so I take out my sketchbook and sit on the very edge of my bed. It starts to rain. I sketch big fat raindrops sliding down my window. I face the window and think about sketching how I look right now— watching the rain fall. I start to sketch my face, sitting by the window and peeking through the curtains.

As I watch the rain hit the gray lake, a chill runs

through me. I still cannot believe that Great-Aunt Ellie drowned in that lake. I wonder if Mom even knows.

My pencil goes off the page and I mess up my drawing. I try to fix it . . .

I make some changes, retracing lines and drawing new ones. When I pick up my pencil to look at my drawing, I jump.

I didn't even draw myself.

The features are the same, the eyes and nose. But the expression is sly and unfamiliar. I drew Great-Aunt Ellie, looking at me with that sneaky smile.

How could I do that? How could I draw someone else when I'm only trying to draw myself?

I try to erase the face so I can start over. The image doesn't fade at all.

I look at my pencil, making sure I'm not writing in pen. I try harder and harder, moving my pencil back and forth so hard that the pages rip.

I tear the page out, but the same drawing is on the next page. I rip that page out. There it is again. I try to scribble over the picture, but it only makes it look jagged and scary.

I throw my sketchbook away from me, and it lands with a weak flutter of pages in the corner of the room. But then the pages keep fluttering as though there's a breeze in the room, though the window's closed up tight.

My heart starts beating faster. I run out of the room.

I hear the sizzle and smell of food. I remember I can't go downstairs yet. I don't have any better ideas, so I stick with the plan. I hope this works.

"I'm going to just hop in the shower very quickly!" I yell from the top of the stairs.

"Did you hear that, Grandma?" I hear Owen's voice from downstairs. "CELESTE-IS-TAKING-A-SHOWER. SHE'S-NOT-DOWNSTAIRS-YET."

"I heard her," Grandma says, laughing at Owen.

The hallway brightens and darkens, brightens and darkens. I look up and see light flickering around the attic door.

"Um—" I say.

It turns off again.

I run to the shower and turn it on, letting the sound of the water drift downstairs before I close the door. I think about Great-Aunt Ellie pranking my cousins and brother. Who's next on her list to prank? Daisy? Whatever she does, I hope Grandma is there to see. I hope it's so bad that Grandma can't deny her sister is trying to hurt us.

I shake my head. I don't mean that. Why would I even think that?

I stay in the bathroom so long I start to feel wrinkly from the steam. That had to be plenty of time for Great-Aunt Ellie to show her face. The air is wet and dense, the mirror all steamed up. It feels like I'm underwater. I shake my head again to rid myself of the thought.

When it has to have been long enough, I turn off the shower, put on my pajamas, and wipe the mirror so I can see myself. The steam frizzes my hair a little and glistens on my skin. It reminds me of Great-Aunt Ellie, having the exact same hairstyle as me. I hate that when I see my own face now, I'm reminded of this ghost who wants to hurt my brother, my cousins, who wants to BE me! I stick my tongue out, frustrated.

My reflection keeps her mouth closed, her eyes boring straight into mine.

My stomach drops. I thought . . . Isn't Ellie supposed

to be downstairs, making trouble where everyone can see? I furiously wipe the mirror clean again, clearing a space for my face. I blink. The image stares back, unmoving.

It looks like if I had a twin sister. The same to everyone else, probably, but different to me.

I touch my eyes, and my reflection does the same. I touch my nose, my mouth, and my reflection follows.

"Are you there?" I whisper hoarsely.

I feel fingers touch my cheeks, though my arms are at my sides, my hands gripping the sink. The face in the mirror smiles.

I gasp and back up, sliding on the damp floor as I try to open the door. I slip but I feel strong hands grip my arms, keeping me up.

No. No.

"What are you doing here!" I scream at nothing, at myself. I spin to face the mirror again, where my face shows none of my terror. "Why are you trying to hurt us? Why won't you leave us alone! What do you want?"

Great-Aunt Ellie is still smiling at me. "I will push you."

A threat? My breath catches in my throat—Grandma needs to hear this!

"You've already pushed Capri! Do you know that she runs track? What if she broke her leg?" I yell as loud as I can, I'm breathing so hard my voice is hoarse. "Why don't you do what Grandma says and just go away, or rest, or—"

"I don't think you understand," Great-Aunt Ellie says. Her eyes narrow and she frowns. I am trying to stand up for myself, like Grandad says, but I don't think he knew how hard it would be. Great-Aunt Ellie may be related to me, she may look like me, but I'm nothing like her. I'm not this reckless, or this cruel. "I've been waiting for this," she says.

"Waiting for what? To take my place?"

She smiles her twisted smile at me.

"I won't let you!" I yell back. "I won't! There is only one Celeste Anne Cooper and—and that's me!"

The face in the mirror changes, and then there's a loud cracking noise, like knuckles against glass. I duck down, my arms over my head to protect myself, expecting a blow to come—nothing. The sound bursts out again.

I open my eyes and the mirror is shattered, a

spiderweb of cracks covering it, and pieces of glass all across the sink and bathroom floor. My eyes—*Ellie's* eyes—wink out at me from each tiny shard. It looks like a hundred of my eyes between each crack. It makes my face look like some type of huge spider.

I scream and grab the doorknob, but my fingers slip as I try to get out. I can't open the door.

I hear another punching sound behind me, but I can't bring myself to turn around again. I bang on the door wildly. "Help!" I say. "Help!"

I hear footsteps, then Owen's voice. "Celeste? Are you okay?"

The knob shakes but it doesn't budge.

"I can't open it!" he yells. "Are you okay, Celeste?"

I'm sobbing now, unable to answer.

"Let me do it!" I hear Capri's voice. "Stand back, Celeste!"

I quickly clamber into the shower, but as I grab on to the rim of the tub, I cut my hand on a piece of the glass. Blood drips from my fingers, down my arm.

I hear three thuds. On the third thud, the door flies open, swinging on its hinges.

I run out, and end up running straight into Capri's arms, crying. She hugs me back and I feel Owen and Daisy wrap around me.

"She's in there!" I gasp. "She doesn't want to go away! She does want to take my place, just like you said! And she's going to push us—"

"What's going on up here?" I hear Grandma coming up the stairs. "What happened to the door? Celeste, are you crying? What's wrong?"

I look at my grandma. I feel angry now. Great-Aunt Ellie is trying to hurt us and she's still pretending that she's not here!

Breathe, Celeste.

"Grandma, Great-Aunt Ellie is here and she's trying to hurt us all. I know that she's your sister and you love her, but I don't think you see how dangerous she is. Please, is there anything you can do? Make her go away!"

I take a few more deep breaths. The plan didn't work. Instead of pranking them, she haunted *me*. And Grandma wasn't there to see it. Now she just looks at me, like she's in shock.

"I heard you talking to her the other night! You thought I was her! She's haunting us! And now look what she did, she punched through the mirror and—"

"Punched through the mirror?" Grandma asks. "What are you talking about?"

"Look!" I turn around and point toward the mirror, but it's as good as new. There are no cracks or glass on the floor. I realize that the hand I'm pointing with is fine. There's no blood, no cut.

I stare at the mirror for a long time. It's quiet, and I can feel everyone's eyes on me.

I turn around slowly. "That mirror shattered," I say, catching my breath. "I saw it shatter. You don't have to believe me."

My eyes fill with tears as I look at my grandma. She looks at me like she wants to cry, too. "Grandma, it's okay. I know she's here, you don't have to hide it from us anymore. Just, please, tell her to go away before someone gets hurt." I'm begging now.

Grandma walks closer to me and takes my hand. "Celestine is a sweetheart. Celeste, I promise you this, if she were alive, she'd never hurt any of you!"

"But she's not alive. So what would she do now?" Daisy asks.

"Celestine is a sweetheart and always has been," Grandma says again. "Fear is the real evil one."

I can't help but realize that Grandma talks about Great-Aunt Ellie as if she's here.

CHAPTER 17

Tears are streaming down my face. Forget this. We need to go home! Now!

In the back of my mind, I wonder what will happen if Great-Aunt Ellie follows me. I'll have to explain the entire situation to Mom and Dad so they can help me. Owen can back me up.

I run downstairs as Grandad comes through the front door. It looks like he has a stack of nature books and magazines, one with a mountain lion on the front.

"Celeste? Are you okay?" He puts down the books and walks over to me. I hear more footsteps on the stairs.

Is it Great-Aunt Ellie? Is she following me?

I whip my head around. It's Daisy, followed by Capri, Owen, and Grandma. "Grandad, I want to go home," I say. "I'm sorry, but Great-Aunt Ellie wants to hurt me—she wants to hurt us all!" I start to cry. "I need to call my mom and dad," I say.

Grandad looks at all of us with a shocked face.

"Ellie? Haunting?" he asks. He looks at my grandma. I wonder if he knows. I wonder if they both knew, all this time. "Is this about the attic light? Or finding out that she died here?"

I don't say anything. I feel too exhausted to tell the story again.

"Come on, let's go to the phone," Grandad says. I sniffle a little bit and walk to call my parents in the kitchen.

I'm sorry if I hurt Grandma's feelings, I think. *But I can't keep being afraid here! I want to go home.*

"There you go. You go ahead and call your parents," Grandad says. I thought he'd say something about not being afraid, but he doesn't. Grandma doesn't, either.

I dial my parents' number and the phone rings twice.

"Celeste? Hey, my beautiful girl."

"Hey, Daddy." I look behind me. I feel like I'm being watched, but everyone is still in the living room, giving me privacy. "What are you up to?"

"Oh, nothing, just watching a little TV. Your mom is

right here, reading a book. Are you okay? You sound upset."

"No, Daddy," I say. "Grandma and Grandad are nice, but their house is haunted and I want to come home."

"Haunted? What do you mean, Celeste?"

"Grandma's sister drowned in the lake here and now she is haunting all of us kids. You can even ask Owen, Daddy! She's been playing in his room and in the attic above my room. She pretended she was me and pushed Capri down the stairs. She threw things at Owen and scared Daisy. I'm tired of being afraid. I want to come home."

I hear my mom talking in the background and my dad's voice sounds muffled. He must be telling her what's going on. I wonder if he believes me.

"Celeste, take a deep breath, okay? You say that the house is haunted. Your mother wants to talk to you since she has spent so much time there. Okay?"

"Okay." I sniffle again.

"Okay. I love you."

"Love you, too." I listened to the shuffling of the phone, and then Mama's voice comes on the line.

"Celeste? What's going on?"

"Mama, this house is haunted. Was it haunted when you were here? I want to leave but I don't want Great-Aunt Ellie's ghost following us back and scaring you and Daddy, too."

"Oh, Celeste. It never felt haunted when I was there. It was always so much fun. Are you sure you're not just hearing the house settling in? Or the wind?" She pauses. "Sweetie, I know you're scared of swimming in that lake, but I hoped you would give it a chance—"

"No, Mama," I break in. "I'm sure. She died in this lake and she's still here, scaring all of us kids."

"Did Grandma telling you about Great-Aunt Ellie scare you? That house is just old, it's always creaking. There aren't any ghosts there."

"Mama, she looks *just* like me! She's pretending to be me! And I saw her—she broke a mirror while I was in the bathroom!" I say. I wish I could send her a picture through this house phone.

"That's your family, sweetie. It's normal for her to look like you," Mama says. She just doesn't get what I'm trying to say. "Baby, there are no ghosts," she continues. "And let's just say Great-Aunt Ellie's ghost was there, she'd have no reason to be mean, would she? That's Grandma's sister."

That's what I'm trying to figure out, I think.

"That's what Grandma said, but I don't think she knows how dangerous she is. Anyway, can you come get me and Owen?"

"Tonight? It's too late to be out on that dark road. It's a couple of hours away. We are coming Sunday, the day after tomorrow. Are you sure you can't make it through two more nights?"

"Two more *nights*?" I sigh, frustrated. I don't want them driving on the dark country roads. Especially since it's been raining so much.

"How about this. If you still feel this way tomorrow, you can call us and we'll try to pick you up early in the morning."

"Okay." I just have to get through tonight, and then we can get out of here.

"Are you okay? Have you been in the pool or the lake at all?"

"Yes. I've actually been having fun at the pool with Grandad."

"I'm happy to hear that, honey. Call me if you want to talk some more. Be safe and have fun. I love you." I can hear Dad saying it in the background, along with Mama.

"Okay. Love you both, too."

We hang up the phone. My heart aches a little bit. As much as my parents love me, they can't understand what's going on. Especially Mama, she loves this place. They don't know what it's like to have someone who looks like me hurting my family. Promising to push me.

I hear a shuffle behind me, feel someone.

I turn around and jump.

It's Grandad and Owen.

"Are you okay, Celeste?" Owen asks. "Are we going home tonight?"

I shake my head. "No. Mama said it's too late to drive all the way out here. But they said they can come tomorrow if I still feel afraid."

Owen nods. I can tell that he isn't ready to leave. But it's probably for the best.

"Are you sure you're okay, sweet pea?" Grandad asks. "You looked quite upset a few minutes ago."

I shrug. "I guess so."

"Your grandmother and I are about to start getting ready for our date, unless you need us here?"

I shake my head. Them being here clearly isn't going to stop Great-Aunt Ellie from terrifying us. We'll have to deal with it ourselves. I remember how excited Grandad was when he was talking about his date night earlier today. Plus, if they've been going every Friday for fifty years, I don't want them to stop today because of me.

"No. You go ahead and have fun."

"Grandma made you a pitcher of ice-cold lemonade to enjoy," Grandad says. "And there's popcorn, too. You can even eat it before dinner." He winks.

I'm trying to get excited. At least down here, I'm farther away from the attic.

"Okay" is all I say.

Movies, popcorn, and one more night. Then I won't have to deal with Great-Aunt Ellie anymore.

At least I hope I won't.

CHAPTER 18

"You two look great," I hear Daisy say as Grandma comes out of her room. She has on a sparkly dress and navy-blue dangling earrings. Grandad has on suspenders and a hat.

Owen and Daisy are setting up the movie, pillows, and blankets while Capri and I are in the kitchen. Capri is popping popcorn in the stove popper that Grandad has, while I'm pouring everyone something to drink.

"Thank you, darling," Grandma says to her. "We'll be back soon. Dinner is on the stove for when you get hungry. Call Grandad or the theater if you need anything. We may have cell phone service there, but we left the number to the theater just in case."

"It'll be nice, the four of you getting some cousin-type

bonding in," Grandad adds. "I hope you enjoy your movie."

I'm trying to distract myself by stirring the lemonade, but I'm still feeling jumpy. All I have to do is sit through this movie, stay up all night, and then call my parents to pick us up tomorrow. We all agreed we'd stick together until the sun comes up and we can go home.

"Celeste?"

I jump, throwing the wooden spoon in the air and knocking the pitcher of lemonade over.

"Oh my gosh," Capri says, grabbing the pitcher before all the lemonade spills on the floor. She saves at least half of it, but the other half is spilled all over the front of my shirt.

"I'm sorry, I didn't mean to startle you," Grandma says.

"It's okay," I tell her. "I was just ... thinking. I'll go upstairs and change." I gulp. I was trying to avoid going upstairs until I absolutely had to.

"Actually, this is all well, because I have something to give you," she says. "Come to our room."

I look at Capri and shrug as I walk with Grandma to

her and Grandad's room. I see Owen and Daisy look at me, and Grandad tips his hat to us and goes outside to start the car.

Grandma is looking in her closet, trying to pull something out. When she comes back, she has something green folded in her hand.

"I just want you to know that I am so proud of you for learning how to swim," she says.

"Thanks, Grandma."

"I know it can be scary, but I'm proud and I know that Ellie would be proud of you, too. And for that reason, I want you to have these." Grandma hands the green folded fabric to me.

I hold it up and the green fabric ripples down: green pajamas.

"Ellie used to love wearing these, almost every night," she says. "I know all this talk about her being a ghost probably has you afraid, but I'm giving these to you because I want you to know that she was a real person. A loving, caring, and sometimes silly person. She would never hurt any of you. In fact, she would love you. You can go ahead and put them on now, if you want, since you have to change your shirt anyway."

What should I say? I don't want Grandma to be even more upset. And this way, I don't have to go upstairs to grab something new to wear. I force a smile.

"Thanks, Grandma," I say again. "I really appreciate it."

She kisses me on the cheek and walks out of the room. "We'll see you when we get back. You kids enjoy your movie." She closes the door behind her.

I quickly change into the pajamas and look into the mirror.

I'm wearing Great-Aunt Ellie's pajamas.

And there is no mistake. I look exactly like her.

As I get the drinks, I can hear the sound of Grandma and Grandad's car pulling off down the driveway. Together, we all sit on the couch and pass the bowl of popcorn around for the black-and-white movie Daisy picked. I try to focus on the movie, but my thoughts keep going back to Great-Aunt Ellie, just snapping back to attention every time Daisy points out one of her favorite parts.

I shiver. "I am so cold," I say, and stand up. "Can someone come upstairs with me to grab my quilt?"

"I will, but can we please finish the movie first? It's almost over!" Daisy asks.

"I'll be quick, Daisy, I promise!" I tell her. "Owen, can you come?"

"Owen is already falling asleep," Capri says.

"Owen?" I look at my brother and shake him. He's snoring.

"The next movie has to have some kind of action to it," Capri says. "And we need more popcorn. I'll pop some after the movie."

"Capri?" I ask. "Will you come with me?"

"Sure. I have to use the bathroom, anyway."

"Could you pause the movie, so we can watch the ending together?" I ask Daisy. She nods and pauses it.

Capri and I make our way upstairs.

"Get your blanket, and then we can walk downstairs and I'll use the bathroom before we watch the end of the movie," Capri says. We both look at the upstairs bathroom. The door is broken from where Capri kicked it in. Grandad said he would fix it tomorrow, but he doesn't want us to use it in case we get loose splinters or nails in our feet.

"I think I'll grab one out of my room, too," she says.

I nod and run into my room to get my quilt.

When I grab it, I look closely at it for the first time.

I realize there's a picture of the lake house on it. A picture of the lake. A picture of people swimming. Two girls and a boy. Probably Aunt Marlene, Uncle Howard, and Mom. Since it's just stitching in a quilt and the faces aren't that recognizable, it could easily be Capri, Owen, and Daisy.

I keep looking at the quilt. Two more girls. I'm guessing one is Grandma and one is Great-Aunt Ellie. One is by the lake, about to dive in. I guess that's Grandma. The other is standing on the dock. Great-Aunt Ellie.

And she could easily be me.

I stare at the quilt. Great-Aunt Ellie is all over this house.

I walk out of the room and don't hear anything.

"Capri?" I say. I push her bedroom door open and she's not in there.

I thought she would at least wait for me, that was the whole point of us coming up together. I sigh.

I walk downstairs with the quilt wrapped around my shoulders. The movie credits are rolling and Capri is picking up the remote.

"I thought you were going to wait on me," I say as I walk to the couch.

"What are you talking about?" Capri asks, turning to look at me.

"You came downstairs while I was still in my room? And I wanted to see how the movie ended!"

Daisy's eyes grow big. "We all just watched it together," she says. "When it ended, you went in the kitchen to get more lemonade for us. Where is it?"

My heart starts pounding. "No, I didn't," I say. "I've been upstairs this whole time." I hold up my quilt.

Owen stirs and mutters in his sleep.

"Celestine . . ." he says. His face is scrunched up, like he's having a bad dream.

"You just said that you were going to get us all some lemonade," Capri says, almost angrily.

"I literally *just* came downstairs," I reply. "I didn't see the end of the movie or say anything about lemonade."

"Celestine is ..."

"Why is he calling you Celestine?" Capri yells.

"No. His eyes aren't even open." I shake Owen. "He must be dreaming about her."

"Celestine is here," he mutters.

"Hey, wake him up!" Capri says. "He's kind of scaring me!"

"Owen, get up!" I push him a little too hard and he falls on the floor.

He wakes up. "What's going on?"

"You were saying 'Celestine is here' over and over again in your dreams," I say.

"I was?"

I nod quickly. "Were you dreaming about Aunt Ellie?"

"No ... I don't remember dreaming about anything."

Lightning flashes across the house, and a big boom of thunder follows it. Daisy jumps a little.

I hear glasses clink together in the kitchen. We all look at one another.

"Wait a minute!" I yell. "Who's in the kitchen?"

Thunder booms through the house again.

Daisy screams.

We hear footsteps come through the kitchen and I see my reflection, wearing soft green pajamas, holding two glasses of lemonade and a big smile.

"Lemonade, anyone?" she says.

She looks at me and screams.

"Everybody, run!" the girl says. "The ghost! It's Great-Aunt Ellie!"

And she's pointing directly at me.

CHAPTER 19

"It's Great-Aunt Ellie!" I yell. "Let's get out of here!"

"No!" she says, turning to face the others. "Don't you see what she's doing? Everybody, quick, come with me!"

I look at her as thunder rumbles around us again. She's standing there with a fearful expression . . . except that I can see the corners of her mouth turning up with a smirk.

"What are you doing here?" I ask her. "Why are you bothering us? Leave us alone!"

"What are *you* doing here?" she parrots back at me. "Why are you bothering us? Leave us alone!"

Capri is standing by the television in shock. Daisy is covering her mouth. Owen looks back and forth from me to Ellie in the dim light. His eyes are wide and he opens his mouth and closes it.

"Owen! Capri, Daisy! Get away from her! Let's get out of here," I say. I run to the front door, but everyone looks at me.

"Don't listen to her," Ellie says urgently. She backs away, widening her eyes at me as though I'm the threat.

"But—which—" Owen points to me and her.

We both step toward him at the exact same time.

"Come on, Owen," I say, moving toward him, holding my hand out.

Owen freezes in place, looking back and forth between us.

"Owen!" I yell. "It's me—Celeste! You have to know your sister! Right?"

"Of course! I'm sorry, it's just really hard to see both of you!" he says. He stands up and takes a step closer to me.

"Owen, wait. Who would know about your fear of hiking and mountain lions?" Aunt Ellie says. "*Me*, your sister. Right?"

Owen freezes. "Uhh—" He steps back again.

"You passed your swimming test!" I scream. "Your

favorite food is spaghetti! You broke your glasses last year!"

Owen takes another step toward me.

"What do you want from us?" I say.

My mind spins. What if Capri is right, and Ellie tries to take my brother and my cousins and lock me up in the attic?

"Celeste?" Capri says. Ellie and I turn to look at her.

"Stop it!" I say. I don't know why she's doing this!

Capri looks at us, back and forth, her eyes getting wider and wider.

"Capri, we were just upstairs together!" I say.

"I came downstairs with you after you got your quilt!" Great-Aunt Ellie finishes.

"I—I—" Capri looks back and forth from me to Great-Aunt Ellie again. "I just don't want to say the wrong thing and get the real Celeste hurt!" Tears fall out of her eyes.

I look around at Owen and Capri. They look back and forth from me to Great-Aunt Ellie. I look at her. Her hair is still braided exactly how Capri braided mine.

"Wait, where's Daisy?" I ask. "Daisy!"

"I'm right here," Daisy says. She was hiding behind the couch. "I was praying, like Grandma said. Because I know one of you is probably a bad ghost. I needed the protection."

"But you know I'm not the ghost, right? We need to get out of here if Great-Aunt Ellie tries to hurt us!"

"Stop this!" Great-Aunt Ellie says. "Capri, tell them that I'm really Celeste! Tell them!"

There's a long pause while Capri looks back and forth from me to Great-Aunt Ellie.

"I think—" Owen starts.

"No! Capri has to do it!" Great-Aunt Ellie says.

"Why?" says Daisy, narrowing her eyes.

Capri looks back and forth from me to Great-Aunt Ellie. Then she sighs. She points a shaky finger at Great-Aunt Ellie. "That's Celeste."

"HA!" Great-Aunt Ellie cackles.

"What?" I say. My eyes sting with tears. "No! How could you?"

Capri takes in Great-Aunt Ellie's cackle, my tears. Daisy is shaking her head. Owen is looking at me with wide eyes.

Capri's eyes narrow. "Run!" she says.

We all run to the front door. I turn the knob, but it's stuck. Capri pushes it, kicks it, but nothing happens.

We hear footsteps. Great-Aunt Ellie is walking toward us, still with the lemonade in her hands.

"Leave my sister alone," Owen says.

"No, Owen!" Great-Aunt Ellie says. "I'm your sister! It's me, Celeste!"

"No, you're not!" Capri says, her voice shaking. "Because when I said you were really Celeste, you laughed in a mean way. And that's not how Celeste would act."

She lunges forward and grabs Great-Aunt Ellie's arm, the way she did when we were all in my room. Her hand goes straight through it, making Great-Aunt Ellie's arm ripple like water. She jumps back. "See?!"

The lights flicker off. Now Daisy starts to cry.

"Just leave us alone, Great-Aunt Ellie, please!" I say. "What do you want from us?"

It's too dark to make her out. We all huddle together and I wait for her to strike us. There's nowhere for us to go, nothing we can do.

"How's this for a hint?" she says. My heart thumps. She throws the glasses of lemonade on us. Then the windows blow open and cold rain blows in, splashing on the television. The television makes a loud crack and sparks fly from behind it.

Thunder booms again and the lights flicker. When it comes back on, she's gone.

"Where is she?" Owen yells.

We look around. I notice the windows are still open. "Let's climb out of here!" I yell.

Capri grabs Grandad's car keys off a hook by the front door. We help one another through the windows, stumbling out. We run through the mud and the rain to the Jeep and pile in.

Capri takes a deep breath and closes her eyes. Then she starts the car.

"Where are we going?" Daisy asks.

"I don't know, I don't know, I don't know," she says, rubbing her hands on her legs and drumming the steering wheel a few times. "Everybody, put on your seat belts!" She doesn't wait to see if we're fully buckled before pulling out of the driveway and down the dirt road that leads us away from the house. The windshield wipers are flashing, and the road is so bumpy, we are bouncing up and down.

That's when Great-Aunt Ellie jumps in front of us on the dirt road.

A scream rings out—I don't know if it's her or one of us.

The shadows on her face make her look like the jagged drawing I drew of her earlier. It looks like a mean and haunted version of my own face.

"Don't leave!" Great-Aunt Ellie yells.

"Stop the car!" Owen says.

"No! Don't stop!" I yell.

"You'll hurt her!" Daisy says.

"I don't know if you can hurt a ghost!" Capri says. The car reverses so fast, I jerk forward, the seat belt stopping me from hitting my knees.

"Hold on!" Capri says. She looks nervous, but focused.

We reverse all the way back to the house. She turns the car around and it feels like we lean all the way to one side, driving on two wheels. She drives into the backyard, makes a left, and goes driving down the trail into the woods.

"There's a way to get into town through here," yells Capri. "Grandad showed me." Outside the windows, I see the shadowy forms of trees zipping by in a blur. The woods are closing in around the car, and I hope Capri knows what she's talking about.

"Watch out!" Owen says. There's a tree looming right in front of us, the trail making a sharp turn to the right.

Capri reacts quickly and swerves the car to keep us from hitting the tree. With a small bump, the car stops.

The four of us sit there and look at one another.

"Is everyone okay?" Capri asks. She's breathing heavily, and I can't tell if it's sweat, rain, or tears covering her face. She tries to drive again, but the car makes a grinding noise. "I think the Jeep is stuck in a ditch!"

"What are we going to do?" Owen asks. "She's following us! She'll be here soon!"

"Should we get out and push the car?" Daisy says.

Push... Suddenly, the noise in my head quiets. I

think about what Great-Aunt Ellie said to me in the bathroom.

I will push you.

She said that, but when I slipped in the bathroom, she *caught* me and kept me from falling. She kept me from getting hurt.

It clicks.

That's it!

She doesn't want to push us, not physically—she wants to push us to face our fears.

She knew Capri was afraid of driving and not being perfect. Which is why she told Capri to guess who was the real me, to get her over her fear of messing up. She knew Owen was afraid of mountain lions and hiking, and here we are, on this trail in the woods. She talked to Daisy about her fear of the power going out and someone getting hurt in a storm. The lights flickered constantly at the lake house, threatening to stay out for good. And even though Capri *did* get hurt—I don't even think Great-Aunt Ellie pushed her down the stairs because . . . I take a deep breath. It's true what Grandma said. Ellie wouldn't hurt us. Not on purpose.

I think back to when she rocked the dock on the lake, trying to get me into the water. She wanted me to face my fear. To swim.

But you can't push people to do things they're not ready to do. Even if they're good things. Not like this. That's what Great-Aunt Ellie needs to realize.

And I'm going to be the one to show her.

"I think I know," I say. "We have to get out of the car."

"Why?" Capri asks.

"We're going to hike back to the house."

"*What?*" Owen says.

I tell them my thoughts.

"Owen, are you comfortable hiking?" I ask him. "If not—"

"I will try it." He takes a deep breath. "If you think it will make her leave us alone. Grandad has been bringing me books about nature and hiking and lions all week. Maybe I can apply what I've learned."

We all look at one another.

"We don't have any other choice," Daisy says. "Let's try it."

"We need to leave the car here and hike back down

to the backyard," I say. "Then we all will have faced our fears. Capri would have driven—right into a ditch." I let out a nervous laugh. "Definitely not perfect." I continue: "Owen will have hiked, and Daisy will've been out in a thunderstorm."

"Not everyone," Capri says. "What about you?"

"What do you mean?" I say. "I've been swimming with Grandad all week."

"Yeah, in the pool," she says. "You haven't been in the lake the entire time we've been here. That's probably what she really wants the most."

I shake my head. "I don't think she does . . ." Could Capri be right? Do I have to go in the lake? Without an adult . . . with Ellie? I can't imagine anything more dangerous. But what if that's what it takes to get her to leave us alone once and for all?

"No!" Daisy yells. "What if she wants to drown Celeste like she drowned?"

"We won't let her do that!" Owen says. "Right?"

"Absolutely not," Capri says. "But that doesn't mean she won't try."

I take a deep breath. "I'll jump in the lake."

Grandma says Ellie won't try to hurt me. I guess there's only one way to find out. But at least my cousins and brother are here to help me.

We all grab hands. I close my eyes and say a silent prayer. I open my eyes and we all nod at one another.

"Let's go," I say.

Sticking together like a school of fish.

CHAPTER 20

The rain has stopped, but the trail is still muddy. We don't even have shoes on.

It's getting darker. Every bird call, every rustle of leaves makes us jump.

Especially Owen.

We hear a distant noise, a light screeching sound.

Owen grabs my hand.

"Hey, what was that?" Capri says. "You don't think that's a—"

"No. Grandad told me how—how to tell the difference between animal sounds. That sounded like an owl," Owen says.

Capri just nods.

"We're almost there, Owen," I say softly.

Owen looks around. "I don't see any signs of mountain

lions. I'm looking for the ones Grandad showed me in his magazines. I think we are good."

Suddenly, we hear a big, loud roar coming from behind us.

"Everyone, stay calm!" Owen says. "If it's a mountain lion, don't run or it'll think you're prey! Look—look it in the eye. No sudden movements."

We hear the noise again. We turn around slowly. I'm afraid of what we'll find.

Nothing.

"Is it gone?" Daisy whimpers.

"I don't think it was a mountain lion at all," Owen says. "Look. The noise was right behind us and the only tracks down are ours. I think it was Great-Aunt Ellie messing with me!" he yells. "Ha! I can tell the difference now, you know! A mountain lion's voice is higher pitched—"

"Owen, I think she gets it," Capri says. "Let's get out of here before she comes back."

We keep hiking back toward the house, careful not to slide in the damp dirt. We continue to walk in a tight group.

A few minutes later, we've successfully hiked down the trail, without a mountain lion in sight.

I smile at my brother. "You did it."

He gives me a shaky smile back. "Yeah, but it was scary."

"At least you did it," I say again as we make our way toward the lake.

Now we are just staring at the water. The storm has pretty much stopped, but with the cloud cover, the lake looks gray, big, and scary.

I'll wear a life jacket, I think. *I'll be fine.*

"Do you see her?" Capri says.

I look around. "No," I say. But I know deep down that she is here.

I walk toward the lake.

"Celeste?" Owen asks. "Where are you going?"

"I'm okay, Owen!" I say. "Just trust me. And . . . stay nearby."

I carefully put on one of the life jackets that are by the dock.

I walk onto the dock, one step at a time. It rocks back and forth, back and forth.

"I'm okay," I tell myself. "I'm okay."

I think about all the lake safety rules that Grandad told me on our drives to and from the pool. The ones Grandma told us our second day here.

Grandad said if it's raining, wait at least half an hour after it stops; it hasn't thundered since before we left the house.

I have on my life jacket and Daisy, Owen, and Capri are watching me. I know Grandma would be mad that I'm out here without her, but it should only be for a second.

Suddenly, the dock rocks faster and faster, like someone is shaking it.

I open my eyes. Great-Aunt Ellie.

"My name is Celeste," she sings. "I'm afraid of lakes! And I don't have to be! I know how to swim!"

"I'm not afraid," I tell her.

Great-Aunt Ellie smiles a sneaky smile. "Well, why don't you prove it?"

Just as I suspect, she runs toward me.

"Celeste, watch out!" Capri yells.

"Are you scared yet?" She's still running toward me.

"Celeste!" Owen yells. "Get away from her, she's going to try to push you in!"

No, she's not.

Because she's my great-aunt Ellie and she won't hurt me.

I take a deep breath.

I jump in the lake.

She jumps in right behind me.

CHAPTER 21

I'm falling in slow motion.

It's almost like the dream I've been having.

Except I was never dreaming about myself after all.

I always thought I was dreaming about myself falling into a pool.

All this time, I was always dreaming about Great-Aunt Ellie falling in this lake.

And she needed to come back to the lake one more time.

I look up and see the sky. The horizon mingles with the water and it feels like I'm underwater before I even hit it.

I hear Owen scream, before all the sounds go away.

I think about the ways Grandad has tried to keep me safe in the water.

Panicking is the worst thing you can do, I remember Grandad telling me. *If you find yourself in trouble, stay calm and remember what I taught you.*

I'm okay, I think. *I'm wearing my life jacket.*

The newspaper article said Aunt Ellie was not wearing one. She probably didn't know *where* to get one. She was just a girl who loved the water and wasn't able to enjoy it because of the color of her skin.

It makes sense. No wonder she didn't want us to be afraid. Of mean people, of nature, of standing up for ourselves, of not being perfect. She wants us to be fearless, or at least do big things, even if we are still afraid. She wants us to enjoy our lives.

Stay calm, I tell myself. I know what to do.

My head pops back up above the water.

Instead of swimming immediately back to the dock, I swim in place for a second. I hear my brother yelling and running to the edge of the dock.

"I'm okay!" I yell at him.

I'm face-to-face with my reflection. With my great-aunt Ellie. She's far away from me, hovering above the water.

I'm swimming, kicking my feet under the water, just like Grandad taught me.

"Swim to me, Celeste!" she says.

I start to, but I change my mind. She's way too far away. I just tread water, watching her.

"No," I tell her.

"Don't tell me after all this, you're still afraid!" She frowns, the same scary frown that she made in the mirror. "Come on!"

It takes me back to what Grandma told me when she thought I was Great-Aunt Ellie.

"You've always tried so hard to be fearless and you've always just been reckless."

Maybe Great-Aunt Ellie doesn't know that I don't feel comfortable swimming to the middle of the lake when I just started to get comfortable with the water. But I do.

I think about Grandad. Right place. Right time. Right person.

"I said no," I tell her again. "I'm not comfortable doing that. And you can't make me."

"You need to be brave!" Great-Aunt Ellie yells. The water ripples a little around her.

"I am being brave!" I feel afraid, yelling at a ghost when all I want to do is go home. I watch her float above the water, a sudden ray of moonlight going straight through her and bouncing off the lake water.

She stares at me, with eyes as bright as stars. "I don't believe you!" she taunts.

"You don't have to."

This is how I will stand up for myself. Maybe that's what she really wanted, even more than me jumping in this lake.

"Great-Aunt Ellie, I like to swim, but I will not go in the middle of the lake until I'm ready, and I'm not ready yet," I say. "It's going to take some time."

She looks at me for a long time. I feel my cousins right behind me on the dock.

"I have always wanted to do this," she says.

"I know," I tell her.

"I'm glad you get to do it," she says. Her crooked smile takes over her face.

"I know." I can't tell if I'm crying or if water is running down my face. "Me too."

She splashes me with water and laughs a little. The scary frown disappears from her face.

"Will you leave us alone now?" I ask her, laughing.

"I'll never haunt or prank any of you again," she says. "I'm sorry for scaring you. But you were all just so . . . afraid. It was so *easy*. And pranking is how I have fun. I'm sorry for almost hurting all of you. I guess I don't know my own strength."

"Did you push Capri down the stairs?" I blurt out. I have to know, to be sure.

"No!" she says. "I didn't push her—I was actually trying to catch her! I—I tried my best to break her fall."

I think back to that moment, how Capri reached back for someone. How thankful we were that she only had a bruise.

"It's okay," I say, letting go of my anger. I picture it floating on the water, rippling far away from me.

"I think I'm done here. I'm going to go rest. But first, can you—" She stops.

"Can I what?" I ask.

"Can you help me swim?"

I look back at my cousins.

"I don't know, Celeste," Capri says. "It could be a trap!" She narrows her eyes.

"I don't want to hurt you!" Great-Aunt Ellie says. "Please?" She reaches out her hand. I see the ripples of the water through it.

"We're watching you," Owen says.

I grab Great-Aunt Ellie's hand, and it's cool, like the lake water. She floats down to where I am. I have three reflections. Two in the lake water and one right in front of me.

"Kick your legs like this. Faster!" I tell her. She does it and giggles. A light sound that floats to the sky.

She looks back at the lake house and smiles. "Can you do me a favor and give Judy and Jim all my love?"

"Sure," I say. I don't know what else to say to this ghost, my reflection. My great-aunt.

Actually, I think I do know what to say.

"Thank you," I tell her.

I hold my breath and tip forward, floating, my head under the water.

I think about how she was denied the chance to learn how to swim. To keep herself safe in the water.

I open my eyes and I'm face-to-face with Ellie. She smiles, winks, and vanishes into a sparkling light. Like moonlight dancing on water.

Suddenly, I forgive her for scaring us. And I know she isn't going to bother us anymore after today.

I pop back up to the surface and hear everyone yelling my name.

I swim back to the dock. Capri, Owen, and Daisy pull me up. Owen hugs me.

"Are you okay? We were about to jump in and get you!"

"Yeah, I'm okay. She is gone," I say. "I can feel it. We all conquered our fear today. That's all she wanted us to do." I look up to the attic and see nothing. No reflection. No flickering light.

"Wow," Capri says. "This is unlike any summer vacation I've ever had."

CHAPTER 22

"Let's go, before they run out of mint chocolate chip!" Capri says.

"Coming!" I say. The four of us pile into the Jeep and make our way into town to get some ice cream. Then we drive down to the lake and sit on the hood, eating it and watching the water.

"So, what do you like driving better," Owen says as his ice-cream cone drips down his fingers, "the pickup truck or the Jeep?"

"Hmm," Capri says, thinking. She takes another bite of her mint chocolate chip ice cream. "Definitely the Jeep. I wonder if Grandad will let me have it."

"I doubt that," Daisy says.

We've been up all morning, enjoying our last full

day at the lake house. After Great-Aunt Ellie went away, I decided to stay through the end of the week instead of going home early. Today, we started with an early-morning hike. It stormed around noon, so we sat on the front porch and watched the rain pour down. Daisy took her notebook outside and wrote a poem about thunderstorms, while I sketched a drawing of it. Now that it's dry again, we're enjoying our ice cream and making plans to watch the sunset before dinner. Tonight's dinner is fish fresh from the lake that Grandad and I caught after our hike. We went out on his boat, just him and me. I actually caught one, too.

"I'm so proud of all of you," Grandad had said as we sat in the calm water and cast our lines. "You have no idea."

We all sit there, laughing and eating our ice cream. The sun hides behind the lake water, turning the sky a pretty pink and orange, almost the color of the sherbet I'm eating.

"Let's head back," Capri says. "I'm so ready for some fried fish."

The next morning, I catch Grandma downstairs alone, making a huge breakfast. Our parents are going to eat breakfast with us before we all head back to our homes.

"Good morning, Grandma," I say, walking into the dining area. She's setting the table and I help her, setting out the forks and knives.

"Good morning, sweetie," she says. "Sleep well?"

I nodded. "I slept amazingly. I have a question for you."

"Oh? What's that?"

"You knew Great-Aunt Ellie's ghost was here, didn't you?"

Grandma laughs, but I hold her gaze. Her laugh fades away and she sighs.

"There's no use of hiding it from you anymore. I did know."

"But, Grandma, why didn't you say anything to us?" I ask her. "Why did you let her haunt us? Or prank us?"

"Celestine is my sister," she says. "I will always love her. Whenever I was afraid of something, she'd tell me to snap out of it. She always felt that duty. That's how she drowned, you know. She wanted to prove that we shouldn't be afraid of the water and that we should learn how to swim. She just went about it the wrong way. She didn't know about water safety or anything because she was denied the right to learn."

I take the plates out of Grandma's hands and finish setting the table, listening.

"I think she sensed that you kids were all letting fear stop you in some way, and fear is a scarier spirit than even Celestine," she says. "I'd feel her presence around here from time to time. I'd sometimes feel her or see her in my dreams. Sometimes those dreams seemed so real. Even more so lately. Celestine wasn't scary to me, though. But she's still a ghost and didn't belong here at all. I know she's gone now. She's at peace. And so are all of you." She walks over and hugs me so tightly. "I'm so proud of all of you. And I'm sorry. I'm *so* sorry. I shouldn't have hidden the truth from you."

"It's okay, Grandma," I say. I'd protect Owen that way, too. "This was a summer vacation to remember. We're already planning our trip next summer."

The lake gleams outside. I smile at Grandma. It's not exactly a smile like Great-Aunt Ellie's, but it's still a little sneaky.

"Grandma," I say. "Before everyone else comes downstairs, let's do something really fun."

"What's that?" she asks me.

I grab her hand and lead her outside.

"Let's do something together. Something that you and Great-Aunt Ellie should've been able to do together."

I grab a life jacket and put one on. Grandma laughs at me, but she does the same.

"For Great-Aunt Ellie," I say. We hold hands again. "One, two, three!"

Grandma and I jump in the lake, soaking our clothes, Grandma squealing with delight.

"Oh, Celeste," Grandma says, opening her eyes. She swims toward me. "You look so much like her, I can really imagine her learning and swimming in this lake. But you're you, and I'm so proud of you."

Grandma and I wade in the water until we hear the back door open and a bunch of noise.

"Well, what's going on here?" Grandad says. Behind

him, I see my brother, cousins, and our aunts, uncles, and parents slowly walking behind him.

"Oh, Jimmy, just come jump in the water," Grandma says.

Grandad looks at us with his arms folded, then laughs. "Well, you don't have to tell this lifeguard twice."

Before I know it, Grandad is in the water with us. I laugh. I am so happy.

"Celeste! Mom? Dad?" There's my mom, with Dad right beside her, looking puzzled. "What are you doing? Swimming before breakfast?"

"Oh, come on, don't act like that's not what we used to do when we were Celeste's age," Uncle Howard says. "I'm getting in."

Uncle Howard runs and jumps in the lake.

Before I know it, my whole family is swimming in the lake, even Dad! We're laughing and playing and splashing water.

"This is the best!" Owen says, swimming beside me.

"I know," I say.

"We have to come back next summer," Capri says, holding out her pinkie for us to squeeze.

"Every summer," Daisy says. We all lock pinkies.

I look around at my whole family swimming and splashing and having fun.

Wow, Great-Aunt Ellie, I think. *Look what you did.*

I say a silent prayer and thanks for our summer vacation.

For Great-Aunt Ellie.

For all of us.

Dear Reader,

Remember Celeste's story about her "failed" swimming lessons, where Stinky-Breath Jared tried to force her to jump into the pool? That was my own story, exactly the way I remember it. I don't remember the instructor's name, but his breath was stinky and he was kind of rude. At the end of the swimming lessons, all I had accomplished was being able to float and dunk my head underwater for a few seconds.

A few days before the first lesson, my mom watched some special on TV about the dangers of swimming. Although I was happy to show my mom how well I could float, by the time I got to my last lesson, all I could think about was that TV special. My instructor was impatient, so I didn't feel safe and comfortable, and I grew more and more nervous about learning how to swim.

Over the years, I've heard people say things like "Black people can't swim," much like Owen's classmate did. Of course, we know this isn't true for every Black person. You, reading this, may know how to swim, and may know quite a few Black people who do. But it is true that 64 percent of Black children can't swim, and if the adults in the house can't swim, there's only a 19 percent chance that the children in the house will learn. My mom and grandma still don't know how to swim—and neither do I. This is an example of how things can be generational. How can someone teach their children to do things they don't know how to do? Everything has an origin story, and I discovered a few things that led to the difficulties with Black people's relationship with water in the early 1900s.

In this story, I talk about segregated pools. Public swimming pools became popular in the 1920s, but they were segregated. Some towns, such as Louisville, Kentucky, only had one swimming pool for Black swimmers, while there were multiple swimming pools for white swimmers. Often the pools meant for Blacks were run-down, too. This lack of access meant Black people had less of a chance to learn how to swim.

Pools were desegregated in the 1950s, but some people were still not happy about it. There were incidents where white people threw nails and acid in pools to keep Black people from swimming in them. Riots broke out at pools in major cities. White-only swim clubs and private pools became more popular, which led to funding being taken away from public, integrated pools. That meant there was no money to pay for swimming lessons or swim teams for Black swimmers.

Unfortunately, instances like this still happen today. There have been a few within the past couple of years where police officers were called on Black swimmers because a white person wasn't comfortable with them being there or assumed they weren't supposed to be.

As Grandad Jim said, all these things caused a fear or indifference of having fun in water. Although there are still obstacles, I'm glad that we are working to change that. Like Celeste, any time you are in the water, going at your own pace, because you want to be, you are doing something that many people couldn't do even seventy years ago. I think about Simone Manuel—in 2016, she became the first Black woman to win an individual gold medal in the Olympics in swimming. As Celeste said, "I bet they'd be *super* proud of her." I bet they'd be super proud of you, too.

Finally, the idea for *The Girl in the Lake* was inspired by my time living by Lake Norman in North Carolina. I love the idea of living in a lake town, with the water always visible. I pictured myself writing this story while learning how to swim, right along Celeste. But the pandemic hit and I had a baby, so I haven't been able to learn just yet. Hopefully, by the time this story is published, I will have learned—along with my son!—so feel free to ask me!

Although it's a horror story, *The Girl in the Lake* is also a story of family, conquering fears, and finding your own, unique voice. I truly hope you enjoyed it.

—*India*

Acknowledgments

First, I would like to thank God and Jesus. Many times, I struggled to find the words to write this story and would take a step back and pray. Thank You for Your guidance.

I would love to thank all the parents. I wrote this story as a first-time parent, with a baby just weeks old in the middle of a pandemic. If you are reading this with your children, from one parent to another, I thank you.

Mommy, thank you for putting me in swimming lessons when you didn't even know how to swim, and also always encouraging us to pursue our dreams. I love you!

To my husband, Rob: Thank you for all the support while I wrote this story as we figured out how to be parents. I love you!

To my son, Baby Bear: Thank you for being born, for your silliness and snuggles. I love you and love being your mommy so much!

I want to thank the first-generation grandchildren for being an inspiration to this story: Devon; my brother, Eli; and Deshawn, aka those of us who are exactly three years apart. So much of this story is inspired by y'all!

Can't forget about the younger cousins: Antonio, Olivia, Alex, Tristyn, Journey, and all the cousins to come.

Our Matriarch: Ma, I love you! You're coming to swimming lessons, too!

Thank you to Kelley, Donovan, and the Browns for being an up-close-and-personal look at a Black family that loves water.

Holly Root, for being the best agent I could ask for, seriously!

Emily Seife, for being right there with me in the new-baby stages, for giving me so much grace throughout this entire book-writing process.

The entire Scholastic team: You are a true blessing. I can't thank you enough!

My aunt Annette and her family, the Breechers, for their lake house inspiration.

My uncles, who always manage to pop up in my stories: Greg, Lamont, Shawnelle, and my uncles in heaven, Sammy and Tony.

To the Hollidays: Dad, Toi, Grandma Carol—thank you. Grandad Clyde, thank you for the Grandad inspiration. Great-Grandma Ruby: Part of this book was inspired by those trips to the country! To the late, Great-Grandpa Jim: I decided to name Celeste's grandad after you.

Simone Manuel, the first African American woman to win an individual Olympic gold medal in swimming: Thank you for being an inspiration to Black Girls everywhere.

And lastly, but certainly not least, the readers: I can't thank you enough for your support. It is such an honor to have my words read by you.

India Hill Brown graduated with a bachelor of arts in mass communications from Claflin University. She was born and raised in South Carolina and currently lives there with her husband and son. Her debut novel, *The Forgotten Girl*, was an NAACP Image Award nominee and is an ALSC Notable Children's Book. She has worked for HBO, *New York Magazine*, and the University of South Carolina, and has written for publications such as *Teen Vogue*, Apartment Therapy, and *Sesi Magazine*. When she's not working on her novels, she can be found playing around with her toddler, reading a book, or writing in her (many) notebooks. Learn more at IndiaHillBrown.com, and follow her on YouTube (youtube.com/booksandbighair) and on Instagram (@booksandbighair).